Night Frights

collection

39 SCARY TALES

J. B. STAMPER

SCHOLASTIC INC.

New York Toronto London Auckland Sydney
Mexico City New Delhi Hong Kong Buenos Aires

Some stories are retellings of classic American folklore legends.

No part of this publication may be reproduced, stored in a retrieval system,
or transmitted in any form or by any means, electronic, mechanical, photocopying, recording,
or otherwise, without written permission of the publisher.
For information regarding permission, write to Scholastic Inc.,
Attention: Permissions Department, 557 Broadway, New York, NY 10012.

Night Frights, ISBN 0-590-46046-3, Copyright © 1993 by J.B. Stamper.
More Night Frights, ISBN 0-590-46045-5, Copyright © 1993 by Judith Stamper.
Still More Night Frights, ISBN 0-590-62406-7, Copyright © 1996 by Judith Bauer Stamper.

All rights reserved. Published by Scholastic Inc.
SCHOLASTIC and associated logos are trademarks
and/or registered trademarks of Scholastic Inc.

12 11 10 9 8 7 6 5 4 3 2 1   6 7 8 9 10 11/0

Printed in the U.S.A.   40

This edition created exclusively for Barnes & Noble, Inc.

2006 Barnes & Noble Books

ISBN-13: 978-0-7607-9638-2
ISBN-10: 0-7607-9638-6

First compilation printing, October 2006

CONTENTS

THIRTEEN SCARY STORIES

Contents

Graveyard Dare

The four boys had dragged their sleeping bags and pillows up to the top floor of the old house. They had brought along flashlights because there wasn't any electricity in the attic. Now they were sitting around talking by the eerie glow of the lights. One of the boys — his name was Andrew — went over to the small window in one of the house's gables and peered out.

"Look, you can see that old graveyard from here," he said.

His friends, Tommy, Mark, and Richard, crowded behind him to stare out the small panes of the window.

"You can even see the tombstones," Mark said. "They're all white in the moonlight, like ghosts."

"My dad told me some old stories about that graveyard," Richard said, "when we first moved into this house. He said I should keep out of it at night."

Andrew turned to Richard with a look of dis-

1

gust. "And you're probably too scared to go in there, anyway. It's only a graveyard with a bunch of dead people's skeletons a couple of feet under the ground. Do you think they're going to rise up and get you?"

The other three boys laughed nervously. Then Mark said in a low voice, "Why don't you go out there right now if you think you're so brave?"

Everyone turned to watch Andrew's face. He had picked up his flashlight again, and the eerie light was shining on his features. All of a sudden, a strange grin came over his face and he said, "Okay, I'll show you guys. I'll do it. You can watch me from up here."

"Come on, Mark was just kidding," Richard said. "And anyway, if my parents found out about this, I'd be grounded forever."

"How would they find out?" Andrew said, pulling on his sneakers.

"Listen, how will we know that you really go in?" Mark said. "You could just go down there, but never go inside the cemetery. I want proof."

"Like what?" Andrew said. "A skeleton?"

"I've got an idea," Richard said. "There's that old white birch tree that grows right in the middle of the cemetery. You've all seen it, right? It's the only birch tree growing in the whole town. So if Andrew breaks off a branch and brings it back here, we'll know from the white bark that he was inside the cemetery."

"It's a deal," Mark said.

"A deal," Andrew echoed.

Richard went down the stairs with Andrew to help him slip out the back door of the house.

"Hey, you don't really have do to this," Richard said. "We can all just forget about it, you know."

"Just go back upstairs and wait for me," Andrew said. "I'm not afraid of a graveyard at night." Then he slipped away into the shadows of the big trees that grew around Richard's house.

It was colder out than Andrew had expected. He felt the wind cut through his thin jacket as he circled around Richard's house and took the sidewalk that led to the old church. He was only a few yards away from it when the bell high in the old tower began to ring. The sound of the bell echoed through the night, over and over, one . . . two . . . three. . . . It kept up until it had struck twelve. Andrew's ears were still ringing after the bell had stopped, and his whole body seemed to be shaking. The bell's vibration had set his nerves on edge, especially when he realized it was after midnight.

Andrew crept around the side of the stone walls of the church, heading for the low iron fence that surrounded the cemetery. Just as he drew near the gate, he heard a strange rustling sound, like animals moving in the night or branches clawing against a wall. For a second he stopped, his heart in his throat. Then he looked up and saw Richard's house in the distance. The glow of three flashlights shone in the high attic window. Andrew knew he had to go on, or he would never live it down.

The gate in the iron fence was locked, just as Andrew thought it would be. He had seen a church custodian lock it up at nightfall before. He felt the sharp tips at the top of the fence's iron bars and paused to think. Then he backed up, took a running jump, and vaulted over the fence. His feet hit the soft grass of the graveyard on the other side and seemed to sink in.

Andrew stood perfectly still for a minute, listening and looking around him. Suddenly, everything seemed different. Outside, the graveyard had looked harmless and, well, dead. But inside — inside the locked fence — it was different. The tombstones stood higher in the moonlight than he expected. Some of them were even taller than he was. They seemed to loom toward him, their cold, white marble glowing in the night.

Andrew began to walk among them toward the center of the graveyard. He couldn't seem to find a path and had to walk over the soft, soggy ground. As he picked his way through the tombstones, a small, low stone caught at his foot like a trap. Andrew stopped and suddenly heard a rattling sound behind him. He whirled around, but saw nothing except a large tomb with a carved face staring back at him. The hair on the back of his neck seemed to stand up on end, and his body

4

began to shiver even harder from the cold wind.

Andrew started to run through the tombstones, anxious to reach the birch tree and carry out his dare. He told himself that he was letting his imagination go wild. But with every step he took, he seemed to hear a strange noise behind him. Yet when he turned around to look, all he saw were the tombstones sitting like cold, silent guards over the dead.

Finally, several yards ahead, he saw the old birch tree, its white branches shining in the moonlight. Andrew knew he only had to go a little further, and he would get what he had come for.

A low, whooing sound vibrated through the air, sending chills through Andrew's body. It was an owl, he told himself, just an owl. He looked up at a tree above him and caught sight of the moon. A dark cloud was beginning to move across it. Andrew started to run faster toward the birch tree. He was almost to it when, suddenly, he tripped on a low tombstone and sprawled face down on the soft, damp ground of the cemetery. And when he looked up and pulled himself to his feet, the moon had gone under the cover of the cloud.

Andrew put both hands out in front of him and stumbled forward. It was pitch-black in the graveyard now. Then, suddenly, his right hand touched something cold and hard. He reached out for it with both hands and felt it. It must be a branch of the birch tree, he told himself. He grabbed hold of a thick part of it, and with a quick jerk, pulled. With a loud crack, it broke off in his hands. Suddenly sick with fear, Andrew pushed it under one arm and started to run.

He wasn't sure which way to go. All he cared about was getting out of the cemetery. The strange whooing sound was getting louder and louder now, and rustling and rattling sounds were all around him. He couldn't see where he was going as he ran. Twice he stumbled and fell face down on the soggy earth. But he never let go of the birch branch tucked under his arm. He was determined to show his friends that he'd completed the dare.

Andrew looked up and saw the shadowy hulk of the church looming in front of him. Then he felt his body bump right into the fence that surrounded the graveyard. He had to step back to get a running start to clear the fence. But as he backed up, he felt something grab at his coat. It tugged and tugged and seemed to try to pull him back into the graveyard. Andrew screamed and shook whatever it was off him. Then he started to run and, just as something grabbed at the back of his neck, he jumped and cleared the fence.

He never stopped running until he reached Richard's back door. He pushed open the door and stumbled into the house, still clutching the birch branch. He ran up the three flights of stairs to the attic where his friends were waiting.

They stood there, their flashlights casting pools of light in the dark room.

"I got it," he panted, "I got it." Then he pulled the branch from under his arm and held it above his head.

The room was filled by a horrible silence. Mark, Tommy, and Richard didn't say a word. They stood staring at the thing he was holding with looks of terror on their faces. Andrew followed their eyes up to the cold, hard object he held in his trembling hands.

And he saw that it was the arm of a skeleton . . . its bony fingers dangling down into his face.

Bloody Mary

The five girls were sleeping over in an old house that belonged to one of their grandmothers. The house was big and drafty, but the friends were gathered around a fireplace in the study. Michelle threw another log on the fire to keep it going, and they all watched as the embers glowed brighter and the orange-tipped flames jumped up from the dry wood. Suddenly, there was a loud crack as the wood began to burn, making everyone jump and laugh nervously.

"Want to tell scary stories?" Michelle asked in a soft whisper.

At first everyone was quiet and just looked at each other's faces in the firelight.

"My older sister told me one last weekend," Kate said. "It's called Bloody Mary."

Everyone stared at Mary. Then Michelle grabbed her hand and said, "Look, no blood."

"I'm not talking about our Mary," Kate said. "I

8

mean the real Bloody Mary — she was Queen of England a long time ago."

"So why was she called Bloody Mary?" Ellen asked.

"Because she liked to chop off people's heads, that's why. If someone didn't do what Bloody Mary wanted, she had them condemned to death. They were led to a chopping block. They had to put their heads on the block, and then an executioner with a black hood over his head came up with a big, shiny ax. And, chop! Their heads would roll off."

Screams of disgust filled the room.

"But that's not all," Kate went on. "There's an old superstition about Bloody Mary."

All the girls drew closer to hear what Kate was going to say. Especially Mary. She loved to hear scary stories. And she'd never heard about Bloody Mary before.

"They say," Kate began again, "that Bloody Mary still comes back. They say that if you go into a room with a mirror at night, and you turn off all the lights, Bloody Mary will appear."

Kate stopped for a few seconds and looked around at her friends' faces. All their eyes were staring at her, and Mary's, in particular, looked strangely shiny and excited.

"So you stand in the dark, dark room with no lights on — right in front of the mirror. And you

9

begin to chant the words, 'I do believe in Bloody Mary, I do believe in Bloody Mary . . . ' over and over again. Then, if you've done everything just right, Bloody Mary's face will slowly appear in the mirror. And finally, you'll find out why she's really called Bloody Mary."

Kate stopped talking, and all the girls but Mary started to make scary sounds and talk about what Bloody Mary might look like. But Mary sat quietly in the dark, staring into the jumping flames of the fireplace. For a second, she thought she saw a face there, staring back at her. But, suddenly, the fire made a loud crack and the log broke in two, sending a shower of embers up into the fireplace. Mary gasped and shook her head, as though she were coming out of a dream.

"Look at Mary!" Michelle said. "She looks bloody!"

Everyone started to scream and laugh. Mary had drawn so close to the fire that her face was flushed red, and the shadows of the flickering flames made her face look as though it were streaked with blood. Mary felt her hot cheeks and drew back from the fire into a dark corner where her sleeping bag was spread out. The other girls started to tell another scary story, but Mary couldn't concentrate on what they were saying. Her eyes grew heavy, and in her mind, a shadowy face appeared and disappeared until it became part of her dreams.

*   *   *

Mary woke up with a start, confused about where she was. She sat up and stared into the darkness until her eyes picked out the tiny, bright glow of a few dying embers in the fireplace. At first, Mary thought they were animal eyes staring at her; then, suddenly, she remembered where she was. At a sleepover . . . at Michelle's grandmother's house. As her eyes slowly became more accustomed to the darkness, Mary could make out the sleeping figures of her four friends, huddled around the fireplace in their sleeping bags. Then, with a shock, she remembered Bloody Mary. The story seemed so real now, as though she had heard it only minutes ago. Then she remembered her dreams, how Bloody Mary had haunted her sleep.

Suddenly an idea crept into Mary's mind. It wrapped itself around her brain and wouldn't let go. She tried to force the thought away by concentrating on something else. But it always came back, stronger than before. The thought told her to find out if the story was true. To call to Bloody Mary in a dark room in front of a mirror. To see what happened.

Almost against her will, Mary pulled her legs out of the warm sleeping bag and stood up in the shadowy room. She began to walk across the room, stepping over the bodies of her sleeping friends. Mary reached the door to the study, pulled it open, and walked through. She found herself standing at the bottom of the creaky staircase that climbed up to the second floor.

Quietly, like a cat, she crept up the stairs to the landing. The first door on the right was closed; Mary knew it was the room where Michelle's grandmother slept. She turned to the left down the hall and kept walking until she came to the very last door. Slowly and carefully, she turned the knob and stepped inside. Mary shut the door behind her and felt for a light switch on the wall. For a brief moment, light flooded the room, long enough for Mary to see the big mirror in an old-fashioned frame hanging on the wall across the room. She flicked the lights back off and, like a sleepwalker, moved slowly but deliberately toward the mirror. She reached out in the darkness and touched its cold, smooth surface a foot away from where she stopped.

Just then, the moon broke through the clouds in the night sky and a thin shaft of moonlight pierced the darkness of the room. Mary gasped as she saw a face appear in the mirror. Then, as she watched the face slowly smile, she realized that it was her own.

The story isn't true, she told herself. It's just a silly superstition. Then she remembered the words. She hadn't said the words yet. She hadn't called for Bloody Mary.

She raised her hands toward the mirror and slowly began to chant, "I do believe in Bloody Mary . . . I do believe in Bloody Mary."

She kept staring into the mirror, but only her face — with frightened-looking eyes — stared back at her.

"I do believe in Bloody Mary . . . I do believe in Bloody Mary."

The eyes in the mirror didn't look frightened anymore. They were hard and seemed to glow. Mary didn't understand why her mouth was turning down in such a wicked smile, but she kept chanting.

"I do believe in Bloody Mary . . . I do believe in Bloody Mary."

Mary saw that the face in the mirror had skin that was pocked and spotted with a rough, red rash. And the hair seemed to curl out of the head like black snakes!

"I do believe in Bloody Mary . . . I do believe in Bloody Mary," her voice kept chanting.

And then, suddenly, two hands — two bloody hands — reached up beside the face in the mirror. Mary stopped chanting and a scream started to rise in her throat. She stared at the face of Bloody Mary in the mirror and saw the bloody hands reach right out of the mirror toward her.

The bloody hands grabbed hold of Mary's neck as she began to scream and scream and scream.

When her friends flicked on the light in the bedroom, they saw Mary suddenly collapse onto the floor in front of the mirror. Running over to her, they saw the blood smeared around her neck. Then Mary looked up at them with crazed eyes and began to chant over and over again, "I do believe in Bloody Mary . . . I do believe in Bloody Mary . . . I do believe in Bloody Mary."

The friends looked into the mirror on the wall. But the face of Bloody Mary was gone. All they saw were their own faces — with frightened eyes — staring back at them.

Cold, Bony Fingers

Tomás liked to walk with his grandfather in the high, windswept hills that surrounded the small town where he lived. The hills were cut into strange shapes by the wind that had been blowing over them for more centuries than Tomás could imagine. His grandfather told Tomás about the ancient peoples who lived in the hills and were probably still buried there.

Tomás listened to his grandfather's stories, but he didn't believe all of them, especially the ones about the dead people. Tomás wasn't the least bit superstitious, and his grandfather's stories were full of warnings about ghosts and evil spirits.

One day, Tomás went out walking in the hills by himself. His grandfather wasn't feeling well because his legs were stiff and ached. Tomás promised to bring back a special plant that helped cure the aching. It grew wild in the hills where he and his grandfather often took their walks.

Tomás set off from the town on a trail that

wound up through the reddish-brown soil into the mountains. He decided to go visit the sheltered, cavelike hollows that the wind had carved into one of the hills many centuries ago. As he walked, he was surprised to find so many rocks fallen on the trail. He remembered hearing the wind last night when it woke him from a deep sleep. But the storm must have been much worse than he realized to have loosened so much dirt and rock from the mountain.

Tomás walked on, glancing around for the plant that he had promised to bring his grandfather. But he remembered that it grew much higher on the mountain, close to where the hollows were. As he climbed up the trail, Tomás hugged his jacket tighter around his body. The wind was still blowing hard, and it cut through his clothes like a knife. Tomás started to run to stay warm. Soon, he came to an overlook and stopped to rest.

Below him in the valley, Tomás saw his town. It looked so small and unimportant from where he stood. And, suddenly, Tomás felt small and unimportant, too, all alone on the mountain. He shivered and thought about turning around and running back home. But he remembered the plant he'd promised to get his grandfather and started back up the mountain trail.

A short time later, Tomás came to the place where another small trail led off toward the hollowed-out caves in the side of the mountain. He could see that the windstorm had been even stronger here. Loose soil and rock were blown into piles where they'd never been before.

Finally, Tomás reached the base of one of the hollows. It looked like a dark mouth carved into the side of the mountain. He began to climb up a steep rise to its entrance, but halfway up he came to a sudden stop.

Right in front of him on the trail was a white object. It was so white that it seemed to be shining in the sun. Tomás stared at it in disbelief. He'd climbed this rise many times with his grandfather. But he'd never seen this skull before.

Tomás stepped up to the skull and then bent down on his knees to study it. The skull lay looking back up at him with its empty eyes and grinning teeth. Tomás reached down to pick it up and, just as he touched the hard, smooth bone, he remembered his grandfather's words. Never take bones from a dead body. Do not disturb the rest of the dead.

For a moment, Tomás almost dropped the skull. He could still hear the warning note in his grandfather's voice. But now the skull was in his hands, and he wanted to keep it. He could hide it on the bottom shelf of his bedroom closet. And when his friends came over, he could show it to them. No one he knew had a human skull.

The skull grinned up at him as Tomás carried it away from the mountain. He knew that the rest of its skeleton was buried somewhere nearby, and the grave had been disturbed by the storm the night before. But now the skull was his. And, after all, whomever it belonged to was long, long dead.

When Tomás came near his house, he pushed the skull under his jacket and then hurried into his room and hid it. Then he came out to talk to his grandfather, who sat rocking in a chair by the big living-room window. The moment he met his grandfather's eyes, he remembered the plant he'd promised to bring.

"I'm sorry, Grandpa. . . . I forgot the plant. But I can go back to get it, if you want," Tomás stuttered, suddenly feeling as though everything he'd done was wrong.

His grandfather told him it was too late today, but maybe tomorrow he could go back for the plant. Tomás agreed and then went back to his room. He looked again at the skull, grinning out at him from its hiding place. Suddenly, Tomás wished he hadn't brought it home. He threw a sweater over it and shut the closet door.

That night, the wind began to howl again. Tomás went to bed early because his parents had gone out and his grandfather had started telling stories again. Tomás didn't want to hear the stories. He'd lied and said he didn't feel well. But when he laid down in bed, it didn't seem to be a lie anymore. He didn't feel well. His body felt shivery and his stomach ached, and the thought of the skull in the closet filled his mind with an uneasy dread.

Finally, he couldn't stand to just lie in the dark anymore and think about the skull. He got up, turned on the lights, and opened his closet door. He picked up the sweater he'd thrown over it and saw the skull sitting there, just where he'd left it. It was still grinning at him, but now the grin seemed to have an evil edge to it. Tomás slammed the closet door and ran back to his bed, flicking off the light and covering his head with his blanket. After tossing and turning for more than an hour, he fell asleep at last.

Tomás wasn't sure what woke him hours later in the middle of the night. Maybe it was the wind still howling outside. Or maybe it was the aching feeling in his stomach. But whatever it was made him sit bolt upright in bed.

He sat there in bed, feeling a shiver travel through his whole body from head to toe. Then he noticed the strange smell in the room, the smell of something old . . . and dead. And as he sat there in the dark, shaking, Tomás heard a strange sound. It was the sound of things that were smooth and hard, clicking against each other. With trembling hands, Tomás reached over and turned on his light. And standing at the end of his bed, Tomás saw a headless skeleton. Its long, bony arms were reaching out and seemed to be searching for something.

Then, from inside his closet, Tomás heard a weird voice call, "Give me back my bones. Give me back my bones."

Tomás shrank down in the bed. He watched as the white skeleton moved around his room, grasping out with its bony fingers. The legs stalked over to where he lay, and the cold, bony fingers touched his feet. And, still, from the closet, came the voice, "Give me back my bones. Give me back my bones."

Then the bony fingers of the skeleton moved up to Tomás's head and felt his eyes and nose and lips. Fear choked Tomás's voice and he lay there, unable to scream, waiting for the skeleton to take its revenge.

But the voice from the closet called out louder, "Give me back my bones. Give me back my bones."

Suddenly Tomás jumped from his bed and ran to the closet. He opened the door and reached down to pick up the cold, white skull. Its hollow sockets looked up at him, and its grinning teeth began to move.

"Give me back my bones. Give me back my bones."

Tomás's hands were shaking, but he carried the skull to the skeleton and placed it on top of the neck. The skull turned its face to him and grinned once more. Then the skeleton walked out of Tomás's room.

The next morning, Tomás woke with an awful headache. He rubbed his eyes in the morning sun, and suddenly remembered the terrible dream he'd had. Then the memory came back so strong that Tomás began to tremble. It *was* a dream, wasn't it?

He jumped out of bed and ran to his closet. He searched and searched. But the grinning skull was . . . gone.

The Mysterious Visitor

Amy's eyes wandered from her book to look out the high windows of the living room. Nothing was there, just snowflakes lightly falling through the sky. Still Amy shivered. She felt uneasy and a little scared, all alone in the Morgan's big house. Little Isabelle, the baby, was sound asleep in her nursery upstairs. Amy almost wished the baby would wake up. At least there would be human sounds in the house to keep her company.

Amy tried to keep her attention on the history book she was reading. Her teacher had warned the class that there might be a quiz on Monday morning. But it was difficult to concentrate, and Amy's eyes kept wandering off the page to look out into the dark night.

She must have gone into a daze, staring out the window at the lightly falling snowflakes. Because, suddenly, every muscle in her body jumped when she heard the sound of the front door opening.

Amy listened to the click of the latch and then the slight creak of the heavy door as it moved. She even felt a cold draft move through the living room just as she heard the door shut again.

"Mrs. Morgan?" she called out in a frightened voice. "Mr. Morgan?"

There was no answer. Only a dead silence in the big house.

Amy felt her heart begin to pound. Could it have been the wind that pushed the door open and closed? Or had someone come into the house?

Amy shrank into a ball on the couch. She was suddenly afraid to move. Then she heard something that made her blood run cold. Footsteps. Heavy footsteps were moving across the hallway toward the staircase.

"Who is it?" Amy called out, her voice trembling.

There was no answer, only the sound of the footsteps slowly climbing the stairs to the second floor. Amy was so afraid now that she felt sick. She sat on the couch, listening to the footsteps clump up one step after another, higher and higher on the staircase.

Then, suddenly, through the panic clogging her mind, she remembered the baby. Isabelle. Amy knew she couldn't just hide from the footsteps. She had to make sure the baby was all right.

Standing up on trembling legs, Amy began to creep quietly across the living room toward the hallway. Just as she peeked around the corner of the doorway, she heard the footsteps reach the top of the stairs and begin to move across the upstairs floor. Then they stopped.

Amy froze where she stood. Terrible thoughts flew through her mind. She knew she couldn't wait any longer. She had to go up and check on Isabelle. Amy pushed the thought of the footsteps out of her mind and raced up the staircase as fast as she could climb the steps. Her heart was pounding, and her breath was coming in short gasps by the time she got to the top. Several lights were turned on in the hallway, and Amy searched every doorway and corner. But she saw no one there.

Quickly, she dashed to the doorway of Isabelle's room. She flicked on the light and looked around. The room was empty except for the baby, and she was cuddled in one corner of her crib, sound asleep. Amy strained her ears. There was no sound except for Isabelle's light breathing. No footsteps. No hints of danger.

For a second, Amy wondered if it had all been her imagination. Had she really heard the door open? Had she really heard the footsteps on the stairs? Maybe she had fallen asleep and it had been part of a bad dream.

Amy looked at the baby one more time and then turned off the light. She tried to walk slowly down the hallway to the stairs, but halfway there she began to run, and she scrambled down the stairs so fast that she almost fell. Finally, she ran into the living room and jumped back onto the sofa, curling her feet under her. She felt as though she'd just had a terrible nightmare, but now it was over.

With trembling hands, Amy picked up her book again. But a second later, she heard the sound. The sound of the footsteps. They were coming back down the stairs. Clump. Clump. Clump.

Amy wanted to scream out, but her throat had gone dry and tight. She listened to the footsteps get louder and louder as they came closer and closer to the hallway. In horror, she turned to look through the doorway to the staircase. The footsteps sounded as if they had just reached the bottom of the steps and were coming across the hallway toward her. But she could see nothing, nothing at all.

Amy fixed her eyes on that terrifying, empty space where the footsteps had stopped, just at the doorway to the living room where she sat. For several agonizing moments, there was silence.

Then the footsteps turned away and walked toward the front door. The door latch clicked and, once again, the solid wooden door swung open. Amy heard the heavy footsteps walk outside. Then the door shut . . . and the house was filled with silence.

Slowly, Amy stood up and began to walk toward the front door. She walked over to the place at the doorway where the footsteps had waited.

Then she went to the front door and slowly, carefully opened it. The snow was swirling down in big, thick flakes now.

Amy looked down at the sidewalk. In the snow she saw large, deep footprints — walking away from the house.

The Witch's Paw

The winter days were long and lonely in the Tennessee hills, but the nights were even longer. Matt lived on a remote farm in a deep valley surrounded by mountains that hunched up against the sky. One night, he sat around the fireplace with his father and Jeb Adams, a neighbor who had come to visit. His mother and Mrs. Adams were busy in the kitchen.

"It's that time again," Jeb said, "when the witch-cat starts to prowl."

Matt turned his eyes from the fire to stare at Jeb's face and then his father's. He saw that his father had raised his eyebrows at Jeb, as a signal to be quiet.

"The boy should know," Jeb said. "Especially with you and his mother going off to the state capital next week. He should know about the witch-cat."

Just then Matt's mother came into the room

with Mrs. Adams, whose sharp green eyes measured Matt up and down.

"Time to go home," she announced. "We'll be back soon enough to pick up Matt when you take your trip to the capital."

As soon as the Adamses left, Matt followed his father outside to the stable. He had to feed the new colt his father had given him. And he also wanted to hear about the witch-cat.

"Your mother doesn't want you to know about this, boy," his father said. "But maybe Jeb's right. This witch has been prowling around these hills for over twenty years. I say prowling because she changes shape from a woman into a big, black cat. This is not a natural-size cat, mind you, but a big, black cat the size of a hunting dog. People who've seen the witch say her eyes glow yellow in the night and her teeth are like fangs. The witch-cat kills livestock, even horses."

Matt's father stopped when he saw Matt staring down at the small colt.

"We'll only be gone two days," he said. "Don't you worry yourself."

On the day his parents left, Mrs. Adams came to the house without Jeb. She told Matt that her husband was too busy with his livestock to come over and get him. They'd decided she would stay the night with Matt at his house.

Matt didn't like the idea. But since his parents were already on their way, he couldn't do anything about it. He spent the day doing his chores and, that night, he sat around the fire with Mrs. Adams. For a March night, it had gotten very cold with a gusty wind whipping around the sides of the house.

"Hear about the witch-cat?" Mrs. Adams suddenly said. "It's prowling around again."

"Where?" Matt asked, hoping his voice wasn't shaking.

"On the other side of Pepper Hill, last night," Mrs. Adams said. "It killed a calf."

Matt shivered and pulled his wool sweater tighter around his neck. He thought of the little colt alone in the stable outside.

Mrs. Adams suddenly yawned and stretched her arms and legs. She told Matt that she was ready to turn in for the night. But he noticed that her eyes were bright and shiny, like she wasn't tired at all. Still, he got ready to go to bed. She watched as he climbed the flight of wooden steps up into the loft bedroom. Then he heard her close the door to his parents' bedroom where she was sleeping.

Matt couldn't go to sleep, no matter how many sheep he counted. The wind was whining and moaning now, and the glass rattled in the windowpanes. Then a sound came out of the night that made his blood run cold.

It was the meow of a cat. But it was so loud that Matt heard it over the moaning of the wind.

29

The meowing kept on and on, moving around the outside of the house. Matt raised himself up on his trembling elbows and turned his head toward the small window that looked out over the barnyard.

It was there in the moonlight, the shadowy shape of a huge, black cat. Matt watched as it slowly raised its head toward the second story of the house where he lay. He saw its yellow eyes glowing in the moonlight. Then, as Matt watched, the witch-cat turned away and began to stalk toward the stable.

The colt. Suddenly, Matt knew what the witch-cat was after. It wanted his colt. He jumped up and pulled on his clothes and boots. He scrambled down the steps and called out Mrs. Adams's name. But there was no answer.

Just then, Matt heard a terrible screech from the witch-cat, closer now to the colt's stable. He pulled on a jacket and reached for the big hunting knife that his father kept by the door. Grabbing it tightly, he pulled open the door.

The March wind cut into his face as Matt rushed across the barnyard toward the stable. As he drew closer, he saw that the stable door was standing open. He swallowed the lump of fear that had risen in his throat and crept inside.

The moonlight was shining down through a window into the colt's pen. Matt saw the colt, cowering in a corner. In front of it was the big witch-cat. Its long, sharp fangs glistened as it snarled at the colt.

Just as the witch-cat leapt forward, Matt lunged at it with his hunting knife. The knife sliced down on its right front paw. Blood spurted out. Matt jumped back as the witch-cat screamed in pain. Then he looked down and saw the pool of blood on the stable floor.

Matt watched as the witch-cat limped out of the stable, hissing and snarling. When it was gone, he stooped down to pet his colt. Seeing the blood nearby, he kicked straw over it in disgust.

Suddenly, Matt began to shake with cold and fear. He wanted to be back inside the house, safe and warm. He pulled shut the stable door and bolted it. Then he ran through the shadows of the barnyard into the house. He remembered as he closed the kitchen door that he had left the hunting knife in the stable.

A strange sound came from near the fireplace. Matt raised his eyes to see Mrs. Adams sitting in front of the leaping flames. The sound he heard was a weird hissing coming from her mouth. Her eyes seemed to be glowing yellow in the fire-light.

And then Matt noticed her right hand. It was slowly dripping blood onto the farmhouse floor.

The Corpse's Revenge

Henry Archer woke with a start, feeling as though he were coming out of a long nightmare. He remembered that he had been sick for weeks, deathly sick. He remembered the doctor standing over his bed and shaking his head, as though there were no hope. The faces of his nephews were there, too, their glittering eyes staring down at his weak body. At the time, Henry's confused thoughts had cleared enough to realize that they wanted him to die, wanted him dead so they could inherit all his money.

Now Henry felt better than he had during all those long weeks of illness. The only problem he seemed to be having was a certain shortness of breath. And the night was so dark, and his bed felt unusually hard.

Henry shifted his body, feeling how stiff and cold it seemed. Then he raised his hands, which were crossed over his chest, to stretch them. To his surprise, they hit a hard wooden board only several inches above his body.

At first, Henry thought he must still be asleep and dreaming. He knew of no place like this that he'd ever been before. His hands groped around to feel what kind of place it was. The more he examined it, the more he came to realize that he was in some sort of wooden box.

The air suddenly seemed heavier around him than before. Henry's mind raced through the possibilities. He could think of no other reason why he might be in a wooden box than if . . . if it were a coffin.

Through the panic creeping into his brain, Henry remembered that if he were in a coffin, he would be dressed in his best clothes, not the nightclothes of a sick man. With a sinking heart, he passed his hand over the smooth silk tie lying on his chest with his big diamond stickpin fastened through it. He remembered that he had written that request in his will — that he be buried with his diamond stickpin.

Buried alive! Henry's mind sank into horror. The doctor must have thought him dead and buried him alive. He was not dead, but dead he would surely be in a few more hours.

Henry pushed up his knees against the coffin lid. It didn't budge. He thought of the six feet of earth piled on top of him. Nothing he could do would move that weight.

A scream of despair rose in Henry's throat and echoed off the walls of the coffin. He didn't know how he could endure the slow, horrible death that awaited him.

And then, through the thoughts that tortured him, came a sound, a sound of something moving above him. It scratched against the dirt, with sharp, steady movements.

Every muscle in Henry's body tensed. What could be working through the ground of a graveyard with such persistence? Suddenly, Henry remembered horrible tales of graveyard rats. People said these rats were as big as cats. They dug down to freshly buried coffins. Then they chewed through the wood to get to the corpse inside. Henry shook with fear as the digging sound above him came closer and closer. He felt the air in the coffin become thicker and hotter. Now he had to face the choice of two terrible deaths.

Suddenly, there was a dull scratch against the top of his coffin lid. Henry imagined how big a rat must be to make that sound. He tried to push up against the lid, but it was fastened tight. He would have to lie there, like a helpless victim, until the rats had gnawed through the lid.

There was more scratching against the lid. Then, out of the darkness above him, Henry heard a voice.

"We've almost got it now," the voice said.

"All that's left is taking off the lid," a second voice added.

Henry's body froze in shock. It wasn't rats that were after his body. It was grave robbers! He heard a crowbar being wedged under the coffin lid. Then, with a creak, it started to raise up.

"You reach in for the diamond stickpin," the first voice said. "Uncle Henry paid thousands for it. It must be worth a fortune by now."

"No use letting it sit on a corpse," the second said.

Just then, the coffin lid worked loose. The two young men pulled off the lid and stared down at the corpse of their uncle. And as their greedy hands reached down to grab for his stickpin, Henry Archer rose out of his coffin and pulled them down into the grave.

He left them there, screaming with terror. Then he walked back to town, brushing off the dirt that had fallen onto his diamond stickpin.

Coming to Get You

It was one of those October nights — cold and windy — that makes you want to crawl under a blanket. But as soon as you turn off the light, you can't go to sleep. That's what happened to Beth and me. We were staying alone in her parents' cabin, which was right in the middle of a big forest preserve.

Beth's parents had driven into the city that night to go to the theater. They promised to be back as soon as possible, but that couldn't be before two o'clock. I was worried about the idea of Beth and me being all alone in that small cabin surrounded by big, shadowy trees. But Beth acted as though she wasn't scared at all.

Just before her parents left, they threw a few more logs on the fire and put up the screen. They told us to leave the fire alone and let it burn out. If we got chilly, we could just go to bed.

After they left, Beth and I sat on the big bearskin rug in front of the fireplace and played board games and talked. The fire burned fast and hot for the first two hours. Then the logs started to crumble into ashes, and the orange flames died down into glowing embers. The wind outside had grown stronger and was whistling around the house, blowing through little cracks in the walls and chilling us to the bone.

I started to shiver, although I don't think it was just from the cold. Suddenly, the idea of where we were, all alone, had started to prey on my mind. I remembered how far down the road into the forest we had traveled without seeing another house. And even during the day, the trees around the house hadn't looked beautiful and comforting. They were big pines with long, ragged limbs covered with needles. Looking out the window now, I could see their limbs flapping in the wind like ghostly arms.

"Beth, can we go to bed now?" I asked. I knew my voice was shaking, but I hoped she wouldn't notice.

"It's not that cold," she answered. "Anyway, I can make us some hot chocolate."

"Okay, but could we just take it up into the loft and drink it in bed?" I pleaded. "I like being up there at night. It feels warm and secure."

"I think you're scared," Beth said as she went to the kitchen to make the hot chocolate. "Don't worry, you'll get used to being in this place at night. I used to be really afraid when I was younger, especially after that kid from town told me those stupid stories about this place."

I sat on the floor by the glowing embers of the fireplace, turning over Beth's words in my mind. What stories was she talking about? And did I want to find out? Curiosity and fear started churning my imagination into terrible thoughts. Finally, I realized I had to ask Beth about the stories before I drove myself mad.

"What stories were you talking about?" I asked, my voice shaking again.

"Just forget it. I don't want to think about them. Here's the hot chocolate. Help me carry it up to the loft. We can crawl under the covers there. Anyway, it's always warmer right under the roof."

As Beth turned off the lights in the cabin, I walked over to the ladder that led up to the small sleeping loft. The loft was a wooden platform built across one part of the room's high ceiling, which came to a peak on top. I scrambled up the ladder first, suddenly feeling as though I had to get away from something that might be chasing me. I reached down and took the two cups of hot chocolate from Beth's hands. Then she followed me up the ladder.

We settled into the thick goose-down comforters on the loft floor. There was a small window beside us that looked out into the tall trees of the forest. Several of the trees were only feet away from us where we sat in the loft.

"Look, a full moon," I said, gazing at the silvery disk in the sky.

"Oh," Beth said with a sudden gasp. "I didn't know it was time for a full moon."

"What's wrong?" I asked, turning my worried eyes to her. "Does it . . . does it have something to do with the stories?"

"Forget I mentioned them," Beth said sharply. "Just forget it!"

I turned away, feeling angry, and stared out the window. We sat in silence for a while, both not wanting to be the first to talk.

Then, suddenly, we heard something that made both of us stare at each other with wide eyes. It was a clawing sound, a clawing sound on the outside timbers of the house.

SCRITCH. SCRITCH. SCRITCH.

For a few moments, I was too scared to say anything. I just sat there, waiting for the sound to come again. But I heard nothing — nothing but the moaning of the wind through the trees.

"Did you hear that?" I asked Beth. "What was it?"

Beth just scrunched down further under the comforter. By the moonlight, I could see her face. It looked scared.

The sound came again.

SCRITCH. SCRITCH. SCRITCH.

This time it was on another side of the house, by the front door.

"Beth, did your parents lock the front door?" I asked, my voice choking with fear.

"Yes," she said. "And I double-checked it."

I could tell how scared she was. Her voice sounded tight and strange as though she was feeling really sick.

"Oh, no," she said suddenly and grabbed my arm. "The kitchen window. I remember seeing that it was open a couple of inches. My dad forgot to close it after he burned the steak tonight. Oh, no, what if that thing keeps moving around the house? It could get in through the window."

I started to feel even sicker. "We've got to go down and close that window," I said, reaching over and shaking Beth. "Come on, you've got to come with me!"

I dragged Beth to her feet and crawled over to the ladder. As I started down the rungs, I heard the sound again, moving around the house in the direction of the kitchen.

SCRITCH. SCRITCH. SCRITCH.

I heard a choking sob come from Beth's throat as she stumbled down the ladder after me. We stood in our bare feet on the cold floor and froze to the spot as the sound rasped against the outside wall of the house again, this time nearer the kitchen.

SCRITCH. SCRITCH. SCRITCH.

"What if it's the werewolf?" Beth said, her voice shaking with horror. "That's what the stories are about — a werewolf. He comes out on nights with a full moon."

Fear gripped my body until I felt deathly sick. But I knew I had to get to that kitchen window before whatever was out there did. I grabbed Beth's arm and pulled her toward the kitchen. The sound was louder now, coming along the outside wall.

SCRITCH. SCRITCH. SCRITCH.

We walked into the kitchen and saw the window standing open. I forced myself to walk over to it. Just as I reached up to slam down the window, I saw a hairy arm with long, pointed claws reach through it into the room. I was too afraid to scream, but Beth shrieked with horror at the top of her lungs.

I couldn't think with that hairy arm coming at me through the window. I just slammed down the window on the arm with all my might. There was a terrible howl of pain from outside. Then the hairy arm jerked away and I heard heavy footsteps running into the night.

"No, no, no!" Beth screamed out of control as we stared at the place where we'd seen the horrible arm reaching out to get us.

I don't know where I found the feeling of calm, but I reached up and locked the window. I looked out and saw a big, shadowy figure limping off into the night, howling to the moon.

"It's gone, Beth. We're safe," I said.

"But what if it comes back?" Beth said, her voice choked with fear.

"Don't think about it," I said. Then, suddenly all I wanted was to get back up to the loft. I started to run and Beth followed me. We climbed up the rungs of the ladder as fast as we could and huddled under the blankets together.

Beth was sobbing, but I finally got her to stop by telling her that the worst was over. We were safe now.

Then we heard the sound.

SCRITCH. SCRITCH. SCRITCH.

It was the sound of claws outside the kitchen walls. Then I heard the window being forced open.

SCRITCH. SCRITCH. SCRITCH.

Now the sound was moving from the kitchen toward the living room.

"No," Beth screamed. "No!"

I clamped my hand over her mouth. Maybe, I thought, maybe it can't find us in the dark. But we had to be quiet, perfectly quiet.

SCRITCH. SCRITCH. SCRITCH.

In my mind, I saw the hairy arm coming toward us through the dark. Beth was shaking so hard I had to hold her still. Then I heard the claws at the bottom of the ladder.

SCRITCH. SCRITCH. SCRITCH.

It was climbing the rungs, one by one. Beth and I huddled together against the wall. We could hear the beast coming closer and closer. Then there was a sudden flash of light through the window. It shone like a spotlight on the top of the ladder.

And I saw the hairy arm there — coming to get us.

The lights were from Beth's father's car, and he saved us just in time. It's been a long time since this happened, and I'm almost back to normal. Except at night, during a full moon, when I hear funny sounds in the house . . .

This one is a . . . Funny Fright.

Stop That Coffin

The mortician lived in a large, gloomy house on the edge of town. Jason had passed by it on his bike many times — during the day. He always stared at the long addition built on one side of the house. His friends said that was where the mortician worked, embalming the corpses and getting them ready for the funeral home. Jason always stared at the house, but that was all.

Then, one night, Jason was walking home alone from a soccer game that had been held on a field just outside of town. Without realizing it, he found himself on the lonely street that went past the mortician's house. He was shocked when he looked up and saw that big, gloomy house. Jason stopped in his tracks and stared at the windows in the addition. There were lights shining out into the shadowy evening.

Jason couldn't explain why, but he started to walk up the sidewalk toward those lights. He was overcome by an uncontrollable curiosity to look inside those windows. Maybe the mortician was at work. Maybe he would see a . . . corpse.

Because it was twilight and not totally dark yet, Jason left the sidewalk and sneaked up to the house. He was afraid that the mortician might see him, so he went from behind one shrub to another till he drew near the wing of the house with the lights on. He noticed that the shrubs were just like the kind that grew in graveyards — with hard, sharp branches that scratched.

Finally, Jason came up to one of the lighted windows. It was just by the ground and looked down into a basement room. Jason fell to his knees and stared inside. He couldn't believe his eyes. Inside the room were row after row of coffins! Big coffins, little coffins, fancy coffins, and plain coffins. But Jason didn't see the mortician, and he didn't see any corpses.

He got back up, feeling disappointed. Then he saw the door. It was slightly ajar, and it seemed to lead to the basement where the coffins were. Without thinking first, Jason crept over to the door and pushed it open. Then he began to walk down the short flight of steps into the basement.

Right away, he noticed the strange smell — a chemical smell mixed with a sweet, rotting smell. But he just took a deep breath and kept on going. He wanted to open one of those coffins and look inside. There was a fancy one close to the door. It was made of dark brown wood. Jason walked up to it and, with shaking fingers, touched the lid.

All of a sudden, he screamed. The lid had come up and hit his hand. Then it slammed back shut with a bang. Jason jumped back from the coffin. But it suddenly reared up and stood right in front of him!

With another scream, Jason jumped away. But the coffin began to move, too. It moved like a dark ghost toward him. Jason bumped into another coffin that seemed to push him forward, toward the coffin that was coming at him. But Jason jumped aside just in time and started to run for the steps that led to the door. He felt something cold and hard bump against his back. When he whirled around, he saw the big, dark coffin trying to fall on him and crush him!

Jason ran as fast as he could up the stairs. But he heard that big coffin bumping up the steps right behind him. He twisted the door knob frantically until it opened. Finally, he ran out into the night air.

It was dark now, a totally dark night. Jason thought he had escaped from the coffin as he ran down the sidewalk away from the mortician's house. But he was wrong. He felt shiny, hard wood bump against his back again. He turned around and screamed as he saw the coffin looming over him.

Jason ran even faster, faster than he'd ever run in his whole life. But the coffin kept right behind him, like a shadow of death. Jason's lungs were hurting from running so fast. He reached into his jacket pocket and tried to find the small box he'd put there.

The coffin was coming closer and closer behind him. Jason didn't know how long he could outrun it. He tried not to think what it would do to him when it caught him! Then, finally, he found the small box he was looking for. With trembling hands, he pulled it out of his pocket. He turned around and saw the coffin right behind him.

Quickly, he pulled out the thing he needed from the box. He popped the cough drop into his mouth and . . .

IT STOPPED THAT COFFIN!

Nightmare

Before Kris fell asleep that night, she went over in her mind all her plans for the next day. She liked everything in her life to be neat and orderly, and she never did anything on the spur of the moment. Tomorrow was Saturday, and she had everything planned. In the morning she was baby-sitting, in the afternoon she had to help her parents mow the lawn. Then, in the evening, she was going to her friend Jen's house for a sleep-over. She fell asleep thinking about Jen's house, which was an old bungalow sitting along the river that flowed through their town.

The dream seemed to float into Kris's mind from out of the mysterious shadows of the night. She was standing at the bottom of a staircase, looking up. The stairs were narrow and steep and seemed to wind upward forever. She started to climb them, feeling the thick Oriental carpet covering them under her feet. She was climbing and climbing. And then, suddenly, she stood before a door. The door was small and frightened her, but she pushed it open anyway, and stepped inside the room.

The first thing she noticed were the windows, covered by dark shutters. Little shafts of moonlight drifted through them, but otherwise the room was dark. Except for one candle sitting on a stand by the bed. The candle flickered and sputtered, throwing out scary shadows across the room. Kris felt her feet move across the room, and she heard the door slam behind her.

Then there was a knock on the door and a strange woman came into the room. The woman had a face as white as bone and eyes as dark as coals. She came closer and closer to Kris with her stringy hair falling across her face. And she said, "Sweet dreams . . . sweet dreams . . . " Then she reached out her hands to Kris and . . .

Kris sat upright in bed, her eyes wide open and her breath coming in short gasps. She flicked on the light on her bedstand and stared around her room. There wasn't any old woman with black eyes and stringy hair. The room was safe and warm just like it had been when she'd gone to sleep. But the nightmare had seemed so real. She had seen the woman's hands reaching out to her!

Kris squeezed her eyes shut for a second and, again, she saw the woman's face. Opening her eyes, she looked at her clock. Four A.M. Kris knew she couldn't go back to sleep. She didn't want to

49

be in that room again. And she never wanted to see the woman's face. She huddled under her covers with her eyes open and stared at the walls of her room until dawn came and her alarm clock went off.

Kris went to her baby-sitting job as planned, and she helped her parents mow the lawn that afternoon. But all through the day she thought about the nightmare. She became more and more worried about going to Jen's house for the sleepover that night. After all, she had been thinking about Jen's house before she fell asleep. Maybe there was a secret stairway in that rambling bungalow . . . a secret stairway that led up to the room.

Without asking her parents first, Kris called up Jen just before dinner and told her that she wanted to cancel the sleepover. As soon as she had made the call, she felt better. There was no way she wanted to be near Jen's house tonight . . . just in case dreams do come true.

As Kris sat down to eat with her mother and father, she told them about her change in plans. She expected them to look happy, because they always complained that they didn't see enough of her on weekends. But their faces fell when she said she'd be home that night.

"But, Kris, we made plans ourselves," her mother said. "We knew you'd be at Jen's house, so we decided to drive to the city. We're going to the opera and then staying overnight in a hotel. We've spent too much money on tickets to change our plans. Just call up Jen and say you're coming after all."

Kris saw the woman's face from her nightmare flash across her mind. She looked at her mother and shook her head. "No, I can't do that, Mom. I just can't."

Her parents looked at each other and then at Kris.

"But you can't stay here alone," her father said. "Now just be reasonable. Call your friend Jen . . ."

The ringing of the telephone interrupted what he was going to say. Kris ran to pick it up and said hello to Emily, a new girl who'd just moved into town. She'd been trying to make friends with Kris.

"You want me to come over for a sleepover tonight?" Kris said into the phone, watching her parents' faces light up with relief. "Okay, I . . . I guess so. My parents say it's all right. Sure, they'll drop me off around seven tonight. Yeah, I'll bring my sleeping bag and pillow. Okay. Bye."

Kris hung up the telephone and sat back down at the table. Her parents seemed happy about the way things had worked out. But she really wanted to stay home in her own safe room. But at least she was going to Emily's house, not Jen's. She didn't want to be anywhere near that old bungalow by the river tonight.

Her parents dropped her off in front of Emily's house at exactly seven o'clock. Kris had never thought about where Emily might live, and she was surprised to find out that it was so close to Jen's house. In fact, it was the same kind of rambling bungalow built along the river. Emily and her father answered the door and welcomed Kris in. Emily said her mother was away, but would be back before they went to sleep.

The night passed quickly, and Kris liked Emily more and more as she got to know her better. By the time the clock struck midnight, they were still wound up and laughing. But Emily's father came down stairs and said it was time for them to go to sleep.

Emily led the way up the stairs to her bedroom on the third floor. Kris walked up the narrow, steep staircase after her, feeling the soft carpet under her feet. She tried to ignore the hints of fear that were flitting around in her brain as her feet climbed higher and higher.

Suddenly, Emily stopped on the stairs and turned around to face Kris. "I forgot something important," she said. "You go on up. I'll be right back."

Before Kris could answer, Emily hurried back down the steps. Kris didn't know what to do but continue climbing the staircase. After all, Emily seemed like a perfectly nice person, and so did her father. It was just the staircase that bothered her. . . .

Kris came around a sharp bend in the steps and suddenly found herself at the top of the staircase. As she stood facing a small door, she felt tired — more tired than she'd ever been before. Her hand reached out to turn the knob, even though her fingers were trembling. As the door swung open, she walked through it like a sleepwalker, knowing what she would see inside.

There were dark shutters over the windows. And a candle was flickering and sputtering on the bedstand. Kris walked into the room and heard the door slam behind her.

Then, as she heard a knock on the door, she slowly turned around. A woman walked into the room, a woman with a bone-white face and coal-black eyes. The woman pushed the stringy hair away from her face and smiled at Kris with yellow, crooked teeth.

"So glad you could come, dear. I'm Emily's mother."

Kris began to back away from her and fell onto the bed.

But the woman still moved toward her, smiling and mumbling under her breath, "Sweet dreams . . . sweet dreams . . . sweet, sweet dreams . . ."

The woman came closer and closer. Then she reached out her hands to Kris and . . .

The Stranger

Tara's violin lessons were always in the early evening, and she could easily walk home while there was still light in the sky. But one spring evening, her elderly teacher had fallen way behind with his students.

When Tara finally finished her lesson, she could see that the sky was turning a darker blue as the sun began to set. Tara packed up her violin in its case and said good-bye to her teacher. She knew that she should call her parents and ask them to pick her up. But she had been waiting in the teacher's house for so long. She just wanted to escape into the fresh air.

Tara hurried out the door before the teacher could tell her to call her parents. It was a warm spring evening, and Tara felt as free as the birds winging across the sky. She started off for home, humming the music she had been practicing and swinging her violin case at her side.

It happened almost without Tara noticing. The

pale light in the sky faded to a deeper and deeper blue. The green trees along the street darkened until they became black shadows. Suddenly, Tara found herself walking alone through the night. She realized that she was still a long way from home. And she still had to pass by the cemetery.

Tara's heart began to beat a little faster. She told herself that she took this walk all the time — in the light — and nothing ever happened. But she started to get nervous. The street was deserted and the street lamps ended for the stretch of road by the graveyard. She wondered what happened inside it at night.

As Tara began to walk faster, her breath started to come in short gasps that made her sound scared. She glanced to her side and saw the tombstones in the graveyard, bathed in the eerie light of a full moon. Tara turned her eyes away and stared straight ahead down the dark street. Then she decided to run.

She wasn't a good runner, and soon her legs began to feel like lead weights. Her violin seemed to be getting heavier and heavier, too. Then, suddenly, she tripped over a bump in the crumbling sidewalk and fell forward, her violin case sliding ahead of her.

Tara lay there for a few seconds, too stunned to get up. Finally, she sat up and rubbed the places on her elbows that had gotten scraped. Then, out of the dark, came a voice.

"You dropped your violin," it said.

Tara froze in fear. Where had the voice come from? Then she looked up and saw an old woman, a stranger, standing there holding her violin case.

"You should be more careful," the old woman said. Her voice was weak and quavery, and she sounded more worried about the violin than Tara.

Tara slowly got to her feet, wondering where the old woman had come from. She was staring at Tara, but Tara couldn't see her face very well in the dark.

"Didn't your parents ever tell you not to walk home in the dark?" the old woman asked, handing Tara her violin.

"Yes, they do, all the time," Tara answered. "But my lesson ran late, and I . . ."

"It's all right," the old woman said. "I'll walk along with you."

As Tara took back her violin case, she got a closer look at the woman. She looked so thin in her old-fashioned dress. And her wispy, white hair straggled out from under a veiled hat. But the moonlight was so pale that Tara really couldn't see the woman's face. And she had to watch where she was walking so she didn't fall again.

"I played the violin once," the old woman said. Then she began to tell Tara about the concerts she had given. Tara listened to the old, wavery voice. And as she listened, she noticed the strange smell coming from the woman. At first she thought it was some sort of strong perfume. Then she realized that it couldn't be perfume. It was much, much stronger.

"Could I play for you now?" the old woman asked.

Tara suddenly wanted to be home more than anything. But she couldn't stop the woman's bony, old hand from taking the violin away from her. Then Tara had to wait as the woman took the violin out of its case, plucked a few strings to tune it, and finally began to play.

The first note that came from the violin sent a shiver down Tara's back. She had never heard a note like that before, not even when her teacher played. It was eerie, like something from another world. Then the old woman started to play a strange song. It rose and fell like the wind, and suddenly Tara realized that it sounded like — like the calls of ghosts in the night.

Tara wanted to go, but she couldn't leave without her expensive violin. And the old woman just kept playing. Tara looked into the cemetery at the white tombstones, and her heart began to pound with fear. She started to reach out for her violin, so she could run away with it. But just then the woman turned her face up to the pale moonlight. And Tara saw that it wasn't a face at all, but a skull.

A scream rose from deep in Tara's throat, and she backed away from the woman in horror. Then she took off running down the street toward home. But the skeleton stopped playing her violin and ran after her. Tara ran as fast as she could. Still, she could hear the rattle of the bones running after her. She ran until she thought her lungs would burst, and finally she made it to her front door.

Tara pushed open the door, and just before she slammed it shut, she heard a note — a strange, wavering note — float through the night.

Tara rushed upstairs and went to bed, never telling her parents what happened. She was afraid to say that she had lost her violin. And she wanted to forget the horrible things she had seen that night.

The next morning, Tara woke from such a deep sleep that she thought it had all been a dream. She went downstairs, not sure what had really happened the night before. But when she opened the front door, it all came back to her.

Her violin case was lying there on the step — with a little graveyard dust on top.

Mummies

It had sounded like such a good idea — staying overnight in the museum. But now Robbie wasn't sure. He was curled up inside his sleeping bag right beside a cold, hard column that held up a big stone lion. Luke and Michael were right beside him. Mr. Arnold and the rest of the class were scattered around the big room where they were spending the night.

Mr. Arnold had been teaching them Egyptian history for four weeks, and they had all learned how to write hieroglyphics and how to make model pyramids. Mr. Arnold's old friend from college, Mr. Ellerby, was curator of the museum and had invited the class to spend the night there. For atmosphere, he had said.

"Be quiet now, boys and girls," Mr. Arnold announced. "It's a great favor that Mr. Ellerby is doing for us, letting you spend the night here. I don't want any of you to leave this room, except, of course, to visit the rest room. And now Mr. Ellerby wants to say a few words."

Michael poked Robbie in the ribs and snickered. He'd been making fun of Mr. Ellerby all day.

Mr. Ellerby cleared his throat and looked around at all the children huddled in their sleeping bags. His voice, as Robbie remembered from earlier in the day, sounded dry and cracked — like the old mummies they'd seen in the Egyptian rooms.

"I invited you boys and girls here," he began, "so that you could imagine what it was like to live centuries ago, like the ancient Egyptians. But I want to warn you. The museum is a different place at night. I often wonder what happens in those rooms at night where the remains of the past lie so quietly during the day. I wonder if the mummies move under their centuries-old wrappings . . . and rise out of their cases. I never go into the mummy rooms of the museum at night. And I don't want you to, either."

Just then, one of the youngest girls in the class let out a frightened scream and began to cry. Robbie felt a lump rise in his own throat. Suddenly, he wanted to be home sleeping in his bed — not here in this drafty, old museum with its weird statues and mummies.

Mr. Arnold rushed up to Mr. Ellerby and whispered something in his ear. Mr. Ellerby smiled nervously and then apologized to the class if he had scared them.

"I know all of you will stay out of the mummy rooms," he said. "I just wanted to make sure."

Then Mr. Arnold told everyone to go to sleep. He turned down the main lights, but left a few small lights glowing.

Robbie huddled deeper into his sleeping bag as the lights were switched off. It was almost pitch-dark in the corner where he and his friends lay. But Robbie could see the lumpy shadows of the other children sleeping on the floor of the hall. It was strange, but in the dim light, they almost looked like mummies.

Robbie woke with a start, bumping his head against the stone column he was sleeping beside. In a panic, he looked around him and saw the dim lights and huddled bodies on the floor of the museum. He'd been having a dream, a horrible dream about Mr. Ellerby taking him into the Egyptian Land of the Dead.

For long seconds, the spookily lit hall seemed no more real to Robbie than his dream had been. He couldn't understand where he was. Then, as the sleep cleared from his brain, he realized that he was in the museum. And he had a problem. He had to find a rest room.

Robbie squirmed out of his sleeping bag and

crept across the cold marble floor, searching for Mr. Arnold. Mr. Arnold had said that anyone should wake him during the night if they had to go to the rest room. Robbie peered at one sleeping body after another, but none of them was Mr. Arnold. Maybe, Robbie thought, Mr. Arnold had taken someone else to the rest room. He'd probably meet them on the way.

Robbie started down the long corridor toward the rest room. It was lined with the heads of Egyptian kings, their marble eyes peering at him in the dim light. Robbie shivered. It had become colder during the night, and the cold floor beneath his stocking feet seemed to draw all the warmth out of his body.

Robbie came to a fork in the corridor that he hadn't remembered. He peered down the narrow hallway to the left and thought he saw a red EXIT sign. He turned down the hallway, even though the lighting was dimmer. He reached out his hands and felt the smooth, cold glass of a display case. There had been cases just like this in the hallway near the mummy room.

Robbie suddenly turned around and started to run. He didn't care about the rest room anymore, he just wanted to get back to the main hall where everyone else was. But as he started back down the dim hall, he suddenly walked right into a stone wall. In a panic, he felt the wall from one side of the corridor to the other. It was a dead end. Somehow, he'd gotten mixed up in the dark.

Then he saw the red glow again, the same red glow he'd thought was an EXIT sign. Robbie ran toward it until he came to a narrow door. He walked inside a room where an ancient Egyptian lamp glowed with a flickering, red flame.

The mummy room. Robbie whirled around to run. But just then, a stone slab rolled over the narrow doorway he had come through. And standing perfectly still beside the door was a mummy out of its case.

Robbie felt fear creep through his veins like a poison. He looked around at the mummy cases lying like coffins in the room. Some of the lids were still on, with the painted faces staring at him. But some of the lids had slipped off onto the floor. It hadn't been like that this afternoon, when Mr. Ellerby had taken them on the tour. The mummy lids had all been shut tight.

Robbie looked down into the open cases and saw the mummies. Their faces were wrapped in white. Robbie screamed as one of the faces rose up to stare back at him.

Then, as though he had woken them from the sleep of the dead, more mummies rose up. Robbie watched as their stiff arms reached up to pull themselves out of the cases. He shrank back against the wall as the mummies began to move toward him.

"No," he screamed out. "Help me!"

But the mummies kept coming toward Robbie, like an army of death. They closed in on him, reaching out with their stiff, white arms.

The next morning, Mr. Arnold and Mr. Ellerby searched and searched the museum for Robbie. They looked under every statue and inside every mummy case. There was only one thing they forgot to do. They forgot to count the mummies. If they had, they would have found one more than before . . . one the size of a twelve-year-old boy.

Bloody Bones

Nobody in town ever knew whether they should believe Jess Brown's bragging or not. He would sit around the town square at twilight and tell anyone who would listen about how brave he was. He was so brave, he said, that he took walks through the cemetery at night. And while he was walking, he would call out to the dead people.

"Rise up, bloody bones," he'd say.

Then, according to Jess, the skeletons would rise up out of their graves and dance around in the moonlight.

The people in town doubted Jess's stories, but nobody was willing to follow him into the grave-yard at night to find out if he was telling the truth. And many people got tired of hearing him brag, talking as though he were the bravest person in the world.

"Your big mouth is going to get you in trouble someday, Jess," people said.

Jess just laughed at them, although he could

tell by the look in their eyes that they thought he was a braggart and maybe a liar, too.

The strange thing is that Jess wasn't lying at all. He wasn't a bit afraid of graveyards, and he did take walks in them at night. And he seemed to have a strange power over the bloody bones of the dead people in the graveyard. It was that power that made him so brave.

One cold, windy night, just at the end of autumn, Jess set off for a midnight stroll in the cemetery. The moon was full that night, just the way Jess liked it, because he could see the white bones dancing in its light. He walked from his house down a shadowy path that led to the old cemetery where people from the town had been buried for the last two hundred years. There were some new bones in that graveyard, but most of them were old.

Jess walked through the wrought-iron gates of the cemetery, strolling along without hesitation. Ahead of him he saw the lines of white tombstones, looking ghostly in the moonlight.

Jess walked right into the middle of the graveyard and stopped. He listened to the wind whistling around him through the trees. And then he raised his strong voice above it.

"Rise up, bloody bones," he said. "Rise up and shake."

And all around him in the graveyard, the old, dusty bones in their graves began to stir.

"Rise up, bloody bones," Jess said again, even louder.

And the old bones sat up and then stood up and then rose out of their graves.

"Rise up and shake," Jess said in his powerful voice.

Those old bloody bones rose up and began to shake all around Jess in the moonlight. The wind blew them around and made their bony hands claw at the air and their feet dance on the soggy ground of the cemetery.

Jess stood where he was, never moving. He felt big and strong, making those old bones shake like that.

"Rise up and shake, bloody bones," Jess said again, just so he could hear the sound of his own voice.

The bony skeletons seemed to jump in the air at his command, and they shook even more. Finally, Jess had had enough, and he let the old bones crawl back into their graves to rest. He started to walk back out of the graveyard toward home, when suddenly he stumbled over an old skull and fell down.

Jess picked himself up, brushed off his clothes, and looked down at the skull. It was staring right back up at him, its old teeth grinning in the moonlight.

"Rise up, bloody bones, and shake," Jess ordered the skull.

But the skull just lay there on the ground, not moving.

"I said, shake!" Jess commanded in his loudest voice.

But the skull didn't move. It just grinned at Jess.

Jess didn't like it that the skull didn't obey him. He walked over to it and gave it a big kick with his right foot. The skull bounced down the graveyard path and then landed with its hollow eyes looking at Jess.

"Kick me, and you'll be sorry," it said to Jess through its grinning teeth.

Jess wasn't used to being disobeyed and he'd never had a skull talk to him before. It made him so mad that he gave the skull another kick.

It bounced even harder this time and landed farther down the cemetery path. As Jess walked up to it, the skull grinned at him and said, "Kick me, and you'll be sorry."

Well, Jess kicked it again, and this time it landed right near the wrought-iron gates of the cemetery. Jess walked up to it and, again, the skull said, "Kick me, and you'll be sorry."

Jess decided right then and there that he had to show this talking skull to the people in town. He gave the skull one last kick and then set off on the path that led into the little town.

Jess went from one house to the next, pounding on the doors and telling everybody that he'd found a skull that talked. The people came to their doors, grouchy and rubbing their eyes. They all told Jess that he was just telling another one of his lies, but Jess insisted that he was telling the truth. All they had to do was follow him to the graveyard, and he'd show them the skull that talked.

Some people got dressed and came out of their houses, complaining about Jess waking them in the middle of the night with a bunch of lies.

"Listen, I guarantee you I'm not lying," Jess said. "And I promise you that, if that skull doesn't talk, you can lock me in the graveyard all night."

Most of the people just laughed at what Jess said, but one man, who didn't like Jess at all, went and got a big, strong padlock from his house. He brought it along with him as the group of towns-people followed Jess to the graveyard in the windy, cold night.

As they came near the tall, wrought-iron gates of the cemetery, Jess could see the skull lying on the path just inside the graveyard. He walked up to it while the rest of the people gathered around the gates.

Jess looked down at the skull and said in his loudest, most powerful voice, "Talk!"

But the skull just lay there on the path and grinned up at Jess.

Jess remembered how he could get the skull mad and make it talk. He gave it a hard kick. It bounced over closer to where the people were standing.

"Now, say something," Jess ordered.

But the skull just stared back up at him and grinned. The townspeople began muttering to each other in angry voices.

Jess gave the skull another hard kick. It bounced high in the air and landed not far away from the man with the padlock.

"Talk, you bloody bone!" Jess screamed. But the skull just grinned. Not a word came from between its crooked teeth.

The people from town were getting angrier and angrier. The wind was cutting through their coats, and they were tired from being awakened in the middle of the night. So they decided they'd had enough of Jess and his bragging. They slammed shut the high, wrought-iron gates of the grave-yard, hooked on the padlock, and snapped it tight.

Jess heard the padlock snap and ran over to the gates. He grabbed hold of the bars and started to yell at the people to let him out. But they just grumbled angrily and headed back to their warm beds in town.

As they walked away, Jess slowly sank down to the ground. He looked over at the skull. It was grinning back at him with its crooked teeth in the moonlight.

And then it spoke. "Rise up, Jess. Rise up and shake."

Then Jess felt his body begin to rise up. And he started to shake and dance all night in the cold wind of the graveyard.

Night Woods

Carter sat near the warmth of the flaming campfire, rubbing his hands together to work out the chill. It was cold, unusually cold, for October. No one in the scout troop had brought along enough warm clothes. Carter huddled closer to the fire, wishing he were at home in bed.

"Carter," the scoutmaster's voice barked out. "We need more wood for this fire tonight. It'll be pitch-dark soon. You'd better go out and gather some now. Bring back squaw wood, dead branches, anything you can find."

Carter shivered and drew closer to the fire. Why did the scoutmaster always pick on him? Just because he was the newest member of the troop, he always had to do the jobs no one else wanted.

"Carter!" the scoutmaster shouted again. "Get going."

Carter jumped up and started to walk away from the fire.

Josh, the only friend he had in the troop, came over to him and pulled off his jacket.

"Here, put this on," he told Carter, "and thanks for getting the wood."

Carter smiled and slipped on the warm jacket. Then he headed off into the woods. He knew it was no good to look for branches anywhere near the campsite. Everyone had gathered those up when they set up camp in the late afternoon. Carter headed off down a trail that led from the campsite into a stand of thick fir trees.

The trees grew close together, their narrow trunks shooting straight up toward the sky. Carter looked for dead branches on the ground, but the fir boughs above him blotted out the little light that was left in the sky. He wandered from one side of the trail to the other, picking up an occasional stick. Then, suddenly, he turned around in all directions, trying to find the trail. He couldn't see it, and he had no idea which way he had come from.

Carter started to shiver harder than before, and he pulled Josh's coat tighter around his body. He looked up at the sky and saw that it had turned inky blue. The fir trees had lost their green color and were now black shadows against the twilight sky.

Carter knew he had only a few more minutes of twilight before the sun set completely. He threw down the few pieces of wood he had gathered and began to run through the trees. In the dim light, he thought he saw the trail he had followed away from the camp. He ran down it through the trees, his mind fighting off fear.

The trail became wider, wider than Carter remembered. The moon was brighter in the sky now, and its light lit the trail like a silver ribbon through the dark woods.

Suddenly, ahead of him, Carter saw the yellow glow of a campfire. A surge of relief shot through his body. He was going to be safe after all. Carter stopped running and let his breathing go back to normal as he walked toward the fire's yellow glow. But as he drew nearer, he saw that there was only one person around the fire, a figure whose back was turned to him. He suddenly realized it was all wrong. This wasn't his troop's campfire, and the figure before him was a complete stranger.

Carter stopped in his tracks, only a few feet behind the man. He felt scared, but the fire was so warm and inviting. Carter walked forward a few more steps.

"I'm lost," he finally blurted out.

The figure in front of him slowly turned around. Carter fixed his eyes on the man's face. It was a strange-looking face with a long jaw and a wide mouth. Then the man opened his mouth and Carter shrank back. The man's teeth were long and pointed. They were the longest teeth Carter had ever seen! And they were dripping blood!

Carter heard his own scream echo through the woods. He stumbled backward as the man worked his long teeth up and down as though he were chewing something. Then Carter ran off into the woods, away from the trail into the thick trees.

Carter heard heavy footsteps crash through the woods behind him. He ran until he couldn't breathe anymore. Then he fell onto the ground and hid beneath a fallen tree. The heavy footsteps came closer and closer. They were so close that Carter could hear the raspy breathing of the man. He shrank himself into a tight ball under the fallen tree and tried to forget the sight of those terrible, long teeth.

Finally, the heavy footsteps set off through the woods away from his hiding place. Carter stood up and started to run in the opposite direction of the man's campfire.

He ran and ran through the trees with no idea where he was going. Then, just when he thought he'd fall over with fatigue and freeze to death in the cold, dark night, he saw a small log cabin ahead of him. Yellow firelight glowed through its windows, beckoning Carter toward it.

Sobbing with relief, Carter ran up to the cabin door and pounded on it with the little strength he had left. A minute later, the door creaked open. An old woman stood there, staring out at Carter.

"Help me," Carter gasped, stumbling into the cabin.

The old woman stepped aside to let him in. She took Carter's arm and led him to a chair by the fire.

"I was lost in the woods," Carter told her, "and I saw the most horrible man. He had teeth like . . . like . . ."

The old woman leaned over Carter in the fire-light.

"Were they like this?" she said and smiled.

Carter looked up and saw her long, pointy teeth, dripping with blood.

Then, just before he started to scream, Carter heard the sound of heavy footsteps coming into the cabin. And the door slammed shut — forever.

MORE

Night Frights

Contents

The Vampire's Grave

The four boys met in the town park after dinner to play ball and hang around together. It didn't take long for their conversation to turn to the funeral that had taken place in town that day. Everyone had been talking about it.

The corpse was that of a stranger who had moved into town only a month ago. The man had bought a big Victorian house that had sat empty for years. His name was Mr. Von Dram, and he was different from everyone else in the town. He drove a long black car and wore expensive black suits everywhere he went. Gossips whispered that he had become rich through illegal means. But the kids in town had another theory. They thought he was a vampire.

"It even looked like a vampire funeral," Mike said as the four friends sat down to talk under a big oak tree.

"Did you see that black coffin?" Tim asked. "It

must have cost a fortune — and it was as big as a bed."

"I'll bet he's not really dead in there," Kevin added. "I'll bet he's just resting . . . waiting to wake up at midnight and find another victim."

"You guys sound like a bunch of old women," Brian said. "Von Dram is dead as a doornail. He's buried six feet under right now. All that talk about him being a vampire is ridiculous. I don't believe a word of it."

The other three boys stopped talking and just stared at Brian for a few minutes. He was a braggart who was always trying to act braver and better than everybody else.

"I've got an idea, Brian," Kevin finally said. "If you think you're so smart, why don't you just go into the graveyard tonight and visit Von Dram's grave?"

"Yeah, we dare you," Tim added.

"And you can drive a stake right into his grave, just to prove you were there," Mike said. "We'll all go in tomorrow morning to find it."

Brian was silent for awhile. Then, in an arrogant voice, he announced, "Okay, I'll do it. The graveyard doesn't scare me. And Von Dram is just as dead as the rest of the people in it."

Mike jumped up and snapped off a thick dead branch from the oak tree. "I'll make the stake right now," he said. He pulled out his pocketknife and started to whittle the end of the stick into a sharp point. Then he handed the stake to Brian.

"These are the rules," he said. "You go in alone at midnight. You drive this stake into Von Dram's grave — if you're brave enough. And tomorrow morning, we'll all come back to see that you've done it."

Brian grabbed the stake out of his friend's hand and laughed. "Don't worry, you'll find the stake right through that vampire's grave in the morning."

With those words, the boys split up, each going home to his house, since twilight had fallen over the town.

When midnight came, Brian crept out of his bedroom and grabbed one of his father's old jackets from a peg by the back door. Then he ran away from his house toward the graveyard. He wasn't really afraid, but he didn't feel as brave as he had when he had boasted to his friends in the park. The night was cold and he had to zip up his father's big jacket and wrap it around him to keep from shivering.

In the jacket pocket he carried the stake that Mike had sharpened into a point. Brian couldn't help thinking about that sharp point and how it might even go through the coffin lid when he pounded it into the grave. He had also brought along an old wooden mallet that he'd found in the basement of his house. He knew he might need the mallet to pound the stake really deep into the ground.

When he got to the graveyard, Brian easily jumped over the low stone fence that surrounded it. He tried not to think about where he was and just kept on walking through the tombstones to where he knew Mr. Von Dram had been buried that morning. The tombstones shone eerily in the moonlight, looking like ghosts rising up around him.

As he got closer and closer to the freshly dug grave, Brian started to think about Mr. Von Dram. He remembered his pale, sickly complexion and his dark, burning eyes. Maybe he just looked that way because he was sick. Or was it because he was really a vampire? Suddenly, Brian imagined the dead man rising up out of his grave. He might be hiding behind his tombstone right now, his fangs bared, waiting for a victim.

The thought made Brian stop dead in his tracks. But he shook his head to clear his thoughts and forced his legs to walk on. His friends' stories had just gotten to him. He didn't believe in vampires, and he wasn't going to lose this dare.

A few minutes later, he came up to the grave. The moonlight shone down on the name on the huge tombstone: VON DRAM. Brian knelt down on the cool earth that covered the grave. It didn't look as smooth as he thought it would. Had something just disturbed it? Brian felt fear creep through his body. He knelt down and quickly stabbed the sharpened end of the stake into the ground over the grave. Then, he took the mallet and began pounding the stake into the ground. With each swing of the mallet, he thought about the body lying under the ground. What if it was a vampire? What if he woke it up with his pounding? What if it suddenly came out of the grave and tried to grab him and sink its fangs into his neck?

Brian gave the stake one final hit and then tested to see that it was securely in the ground. The stake was pounded in so deep that he knew it must be close to the coffin lid. Then Brian started to jump up to run back home. But he couldn't move! Something was holding onto him! It pulled and tugged at his body, dragging him toward the grave. Fear blotted out all of Brian's thoughts except one: The vampire had risen out of the grave. It wanted to get him!

The next morning, the other three boys woke up early and met at the graveyard. They jumped over the fence and ran as fast as they could to where Mr. Von Dram had been buried. They were taking bets on whether or not they would find the stake driven into the grave. But when they came up to the freshly dug grave, they saw a limp body lying on top of it.

It was Brian, his face twisted in terror. Then they saw the stake that he had pounded through the bottom edge of his father's jacket. He had pinned himself to the grave. And he had died of fright.

The Hook

The four boys huddled around the camp fire, trying to stay warm. It was a late summer night that had turned suddenly cold, much colder than normal for that time of year. The younger boys were shivering because they hadn't thought to bring along jackets. Only Eric, the lead scout, seemed warm enough.

"What's the matter with you guys?" Eric asked. "You act as though you've never camped before. Maybe I shouldn't have brought you up to the mountains. I thought you were tough enough for this trip."

"We're tough enough," Brian said. "It's just freezing, that's all. Why didn't you tell us it would be this cold up here?"

"I didn't know it would be this cold," Eric snapped back. "Anyway, you're supposed to be prepared for anything."

"I'm not prepared to freeze to death," Mark muttered.

"Why can't we go home?" Todd asked, his voice trembling. It was his first camp-out.

"I'm not going home — no matter how much you whine," Eric said. "And remember, I'm the only one who can drive. Besides, I've got the keys to the van." He pulled the keys out of his pocket and dangled them in front of the other boys' eyes.

"Can we tell stories?" Mark asked. "Maybe that would take our minds off freezing to death."

"No stories tonight," Eric said.

"Why not?" Doug asked. "You always tell stories, scary ones."

"This place gives me the creeps bad enough without scary stories," Eric said. "If you want to tell stories yourself, go ahead. I'll turn in."

The four younger boys looked at each other across the leaping flames of the camp fire. For a while, everyone was quiet.

"What gives you the creeps about this place?" Brian finally asked in a low voice.

Eric didn't answer right away. He looked up at the towering fir trees that circled the camp fire. Their ragged limbs were flapping up and down in the cold wind. The other boys watched him. Then they all stared at each other across the fire.

"It's because of a news report I heard on the

way up here," Eric said. "You know how they always make things sound like a big deal on the radio."

Todd started to shiver harder. "Why don't we just go home?" he pleaded.

"What was the news report?" Mark asked in a hushed voice. The woods around them had suddenly seemed to grow more quiet and mysterious.

"It was on that prison about twenty miles down the road," Eric said.

The younger boys stared at him. No one had told them about the prison before.

"And the news report said," Eric went on, "that one of the convicts escaped. I remember hearing about him when he was finally caught and put away. They call him the Hook."

"Why do they call him that?" Brian asked right away.

"He lost his left hand in an accident," Eric explained. "And he has a hook there instead of a hand."

"I want to go home," Todd said, louder now.

"Did the radio say which way he was heading?" Mark asked.

"No," Eric answered with a grim look on his face. "They just said that he was dangerous."

No one said anything for a while. They just sat around the fire listening to the wind whip through the trees and moan across the sides of the mountain. Finally, Eric got up and said he was packing it in for the night. He told the younger boys to kill the fire and then get into their tent. Eric had a tent of his own, but the others were sharing a big tent for four.

The boys doused the flames of the fire, threw dirt on it, and then went off to their tent. Each of them had his own private thoughts that he didn't want to admit to the others.

But when they crawled into their sleeping bags, away from Eric, they started to talk about him — the Hook.

"If he's so dangerous, what are we doing out here?" Mark said. "I think Eric is either lying to us, or he's just plain crazy."

"I remember reading about the Hook in the papers, a couple of years ago. He's a murderer," Doug said.

"I want to go home," Todd said with an edge of panic in his voice.

Just then, a strange noise came from out of the woods near their tent. It sounded like the scratching of metal against a tree. The four boys turned their fearful eyes toward the tent opening.

"Eric!" Todd began to scream. The three other boys didn't stop him. They wanted Eric to come, too.

A few minutes later, Eric threw open the tent flap. His eyes looked scared.

"Did you hear it, Eric?" Brian asked. "It sounded like, like . . ."

"Let's get out of here," Eric said. "We can come back for our stuff later."

The boys scrambled out of the tent and ran after Eric to the van. They jumped inside and slammed the doors shut, pushing down the locks as Eric turned the key and the engine roared to life.

Just as the van lurched forward, they heard the sound of something scraping against the side of the van. Then there was a weird-sounding scream as Eric gunned the motor and the van shot off down the forest road.

No one spoke until they were out of the woods and traveling along the main road toward home. No one wanted to talk about the terrible thoughts running through their minds. Finally, Eric broke the silence when he saw a gas station ahead.

"I think we're far enough away," he said. "I've got to fill up the tank."

As the van rolled to a stop in front of the gas pumps, the boys slowly opened the doors to get out. It was Todd who saw it first. He stepped out and looked at the door handle on his side of the van. Then he started to scream. Something was hanging from the handle, swinging back and forth, back and forth.

It was a hook.

Two Dead Eyes

One night, in the middle of a terrible storm, a bolt of lightning struck the big house where a very rich old woman lived. It was the worst streak of lightning that anyone had ever seen, followed by the loudest clap of thunder that anyone had ever heard. And the next morning, the servants found the old woman sitting straight up in bed, her eyes wide open in fright. She was dead.

It frightened the servants to see her two dead eyes, staring at them in terror. They tried to close the lids over the eyes, but each time they tried, the eyes would open back up and stare right through them.

Soon, the old woman's relatives arrived and started to prepare for the funeral. They bought the woman the best coffin made. They had her grave dug on the highest spot in the cemetery. And they chose the most beautiful dress for her to be buried in. The undertaker was given strict instructions to shut her eyes for the funeral, but try as he might, he couldn't get the two dead eyes to stay shut.

Finally, the old woman's cousin had an idea. He found two of the gold coins the woman had been so fond of collecting. Gently, he shut her lids and then laid a coin over each eye. The weight of the heavy gold coins kept the two dead eyes shut.

The family thought the woman looked rather strange with the two gold coins lying on her face, looking like round yellow eyes. But they all agreed that it was better that they didn't have to look at her real eyes, staring at them, as they closed the lid to the coffin. The funeral service was carried out, and the coffin taken to the grave-yard.

After the family left the graveyard, the under-taker turned the coffin over to the gravedigger to do his job. The gravedigger had heard about the two gold coins that were holding the dead woman's eyes shut. As soon as he was left alone in the graveyard, a wave of curiosity swept over him. What did those coins look like? Were they really as thick and heavy as he had heard they were?

The gravedigger crawled down into the grave and then peeked up over the top to make sure that no one was watching him. Then he stooped down, brushed off the small amount of dirt that had been thrown on top of the coffin, pried open the coffin lid, and lifted it off.

As he looked down on the old woman's face, a ray of sunlight flashed off the two gold coins, almost blinding him. The gravedigger staggered back, and then gazed down in amazement at the heavy gold circles shining on the woman's face. He decided they must be worth a fortune, in their weight of gold alone. Quickly, he calculated all the things he could buy with that gold. He could be a rich man! Almost automatically, his hands reached out for the two gold coins. He plucked both of them off the woman's face at the same time, feeling their cool, heavy weight in his hands.

But the moment he lifted up the coins, the woman's eyelids flew open, and her two dead eyes stared up into the gravedigger's face. A stab of fear struck deep in his heart. Those two dead eyes seemed to be accusing him. They stared and stared and stared at him, never flickering, never blinking.

The gravedigger couldn't stand to look at the eyes any longer. He slammed shut the coffin lid and pushed the two gold coins down into his jacket pocket. Then, like a madman, he began to shovel dirt over the coffin until it was buried deep under the ground. Only when he was finished did he stop to take out the gold coins from his pocket and admire them.

As soon as the gravedigger got home, he hid the gold coins in an old metal box that he kept under his bed. All the time he was taking the coins out of his pocket and putting them in the box, he felt as though someone was watching him. But he knew it was just his imagination. No one had been in the cemetery when he took the coins, and he lived all alone in his little house deep in the woods.

That night, another storm came up just like the one that had scared the old woman to death. The wind howled through the trees around the gravedigger's house and shook the wooden walls. The gravedigger huddled under the blankets of his bed, shivering with cold. Then he heard a strange sound that made him shake even harder. It was a rattle, a rattle of metal beneath his bed.

Clink. Clink. Clinkity-clink.

The gravedigger sat straight up in bed, his eyes staring into the darkness in front of him. What was that noise? He strained his ears to hear.

Clink. Clink. Clinkity-clink.

The sound was coming from beneath his bed. There was only one thing that it could be. The two gold coins from the woman's eyes were rattling in the metal box where he had hidden them.

Clink. Clink. Clinkity-clink.

The gravedigger slowly lay back down in his bed and shut his eyes. It must be the wind making the metal box shake, he decided. But then he heard a sound on the wind, a sound like a low, moaning voice.

"Whoooo? Whoooo took my gold coins?"

The gravedigger sat bolt upright in his bed again. The coins were shaking and rattling beneath him. And the spooky voice was coming closer and closer through the night.

"Whoooo? Whooo took my gold coins?"

The gravedigger pulled the blankets around him tighter and started to shake as hard as the coins in the metal box.

Suddenly, the front door blew open and a gust of wind rushed through the house and ripped the blankets right off the gravedigger. He huddled against the head of his bed and stared at the open doorway. Then he saw them. The two dead eyes. They were coming toward him through the dark. They seemed to be burning with anger and evil.

The gravedigger tried to shrink into his bed so the eyes couldn't find him. But then the gold coins started to rattle even louder in the metal box beneath him.

Clink. Clink. Clinkity-clink.

The two dead eyes moved toward him faster now. And the voice echoed through the air around him.

"Whoooo? Whoooo took my gold coins?"

The gravedigger sat bolt upright in his bed and screamed, "I did!"

And the next morning, people found him just like that — with his two dead eyes staring straight ahead in fright.

The Bloodsucker

No one who saw the bloodsucker ever lived to tell about it. So no one knew exactly what he looked like. People said the bloodsucker was an evil ghost that lurked in the dark shadows of the woods waiting for a person to stay in the forest too long, too late. As the light faded from the sky, the bloodsucker would get more and more thirsty. He could smell human blood from miles away. And when he found a victim, he would swoop out from the dark shadows — and suck every drop of blood out of the person's body.

One day, a boy who lived in the woods — his name was Adam — had to deliver a horse to a man who lived miles away. Adam had set off early in the day, but the journey took much longer than he had expected. By the time he had delivered the horse and begun his walk back home, the shadows of the woods had grown darker and longer.

The birds had stopped chirping and folded their wings for the night.

Adam started walking faster down the forest path, nervously looking up at the twilight sky. He knew he still had an hour's journey to go, and he knew that twilight would never last that long. As Adam hurried along, the thought of the blood-sucker crept into his mind. Just before he'd left home that morning, his older brother, Thomas, had warned him not to travel too slowly. Thomas hadn't mentioned the bloodsucker, but both of them knew what he meant.

Adam started to run down the path, suddenly seeing strange shapes and faces in the forest shadows. The harder he ran, the more his blood began to pound in his veins. Adam reached his hand up to his face and felt the warm blood that had rushed to the surface. He wondered if his blood smelled more strongly now that it was warm. Maybe the smell of it was floating through the woods right now, tempting the bloodsucker.

Adam felt tears spring to his eyes, and he tried to run faster. But his breath was coming in short, painful gasps and, finally, his legs grew so weak that he stumbled over a thick root that snaked across the forest floor. He sprawled out, face down, on the path strewn with sharp pine needles. For a moment he lay there exhausted, too tired to move.

Finally, he turned over and looked up at the shadowy trees looming above him. Then he heard a strange noise, a noise like he'd never heard before. It was coming toward him, closer and closer and louder and louder. It was the sound of something huge, sucking in the air. Adam raised himself up on his elbow, terrified by the sound, but too weak to escape. Then, just as he saw the bloodsucker swoop down on him, he began to scream.

A minute later, the forest was quiet.

Thomas, his older brother, found Adam's body the next day. It was limp and pale, drained of every drop of blood. There was a trail of blood left by the bloodsucker, leading away into the forest. As Thomas carried his brother's body home, he vowed to get revenge on the bloodsucker.

He took Adam's body home and buried it. Then he began to make his plans. All day, he sharpened the hunting knives that he kept in the barn. That night, just before the light was beginning to fade from the sky, he returned to the forest carrying a heavy load on his back. He found the trail of blood that led away from the spot where the bloodsucker had sucked the life out of Adam's body. He followed it through the darkening forest to the mouth of a cave.

Thomas knew he had to work fast. Twilight was creeping over the sky, and he knew the smell of his own blood would soon be stirring the appetite of the bloodsucker.

He threw the heavy pack onto the ground and pulled the sharpened knives out one by one. Their points glistened in the fading light. He dug the handles of the knives into the ground in front of the cave and pointed the long, sharp blades toward its opening. Then, trembling, he stood still behind the knives while the light grew dimmer and dimmer in the sky.

Just when the outlines of the trees had faded from green to black, Thomas heard a terrifying sound from inside the cave. The blood in his veins began to pound with fear, but he stood his ground behind the knives. Then, suddenly, the bloodsucker swooped out of the cave, its huge mouth gaping open, thirsty for blood.

The bloodsucker came right for Thomas, not seeing the rows of blades in front of him. It screamed out and twisted and turned in agony as the sharp knives cut it into hundreds and thousands of pieces.

Then all those pieces of the bloodsucker flew up into the night sky. And they turned into mosquitoes, still thirsty for blood.

And, so, if you're ever out in the woods at night, watch out for mosquitoes. They'll suck the blood right out of you!

Time Was Running Out

The human mind starts acting strangely after a person has been alone for a long time. That's what I tried to tell myself as I lay in my bed, tossing and turning. It had to be my imagination, I said over and over. That sound I heard . . . that tapping, tocking sound.

I was all alone in the North Woods. For ten days I had been ice fishing during the day and then writing in my journal at night. The cold weather and bleak landscape around me was the sort of break I needed from my high-pressure job in the city. Everything had been peaceful and quiet — until now. Now my mind was obsessed by the sound that I had been hearing for what seemed like hours — the sound of something tapping on the lake ice that surrounded my cabin on nearly all sides.

I got out of bed and peered out the window of my cabin. It was dawn and the sun was just coloring the sky with pale blues and pinks. I thought I saw a dark figure moving across the ice toward my cabin, but then it seemed to disappear. I wasn't sure if I had imagined seeing it or not.

I pulled on my long underwear and hunting clothes — parka, insulated pants, boots, fur cap, and gloves. I wasn't sure what I was going to do, but I knew I couldn't just sit in my cabin any longer, waiting for the tapping noise to come to me. If I did, I'd go crazy.

I slipped outside and gulped in breaths of the icy cold air. Outside, the sound was even louder. As I listened to it echoing across the frozen lake, I suddenly realized what must be causing it. A person was coming toward me, testing the ice with a pole. Each time the pole was set down against the hard surface of the ice, it made a tapping sound.

A wave of relief washed over me, but it was soon replaced by an uneasy curiosity about who might be coming toward me in this isolated wilderness. Who was it? And why did he want to find me?

Instinctively, I sought cover in a stand of huge fir trees. I wanted to see who was making the noise before being seen myself. I waited there, for what seemed like an hour, listening as the tapping, tocking sound grew closer and closer. Finally, I realized that my fingers and toes had grown numb and stiff. I was risking frostbite if I remained still any longer. I stepped out from the cover of the trees. Gazing across the frozen lake around me, I couldn't see anyone. But now I heard the sound moving in a different direction — away from me. Somehow, the person tapping his pole on the ice had circled around me and was now moving away.

Forgetting that I hadn't eaten breakfast or supplied myself with food, I began to trail the mysterious sound. Even though it was moving away from me now, I feared it even more. It had an evil persistence that drilled into my brain. I had to know what person was prowling on these lakes — I didn't want to be surprised by a sudden intruder in my cabin.

For hours, I followed the tapping and tocking across the ice. It led me in a half circle around the lake. I was beginning to feel hungry and cold, and suddenly, I knew I had to head back to my cabin. If I didn't get there by nightfall, I would freeze to death on the lake.

I came to a halt on the ice, my legs trembling with fatigue. And as I turned my back to begin my walk home, my blood turned even colder than before. I realized that, now, the tapping sound was following me. It was tracking me down across the ice.

Panic began to seep through my body. It made

me feel weaker than before, but I started to run anyway. Before, I had been curious, and then fearful, of the sound; now I was terrified.

Tock. Tock. Tock.

The sound seemed to grow louder and louder in my ears. I staggered across the icy lake, no longer checking for the thin places in the ice where warmer currents ran. I knew only one thing. I had to escape that sound before it caught up with me.

Tock. Tock. Tock.

Suddenly, I sprawled forward onto the ice. My legs had given out. I was starving and could feel the frostbite creeping into my fingers and toes. But the sound of the tapping, tocking pole didn't stop. It came closer and closer, hunting me down like a predator's victim.

Tock. Tock. Tock.

In my mind, I could see who must be carrying that pole. His face was covered by a bushy black beard. His eyes were evil and hungry. His ragged teeth worked hungrily under red lips. I lay on the ice, unable to move. I knew it was only a matter of time until the tocking sound reached my face, frozen against the ice. And time was running out.

"No!" I screamed. And I sat bolt upright. Looking around me, I saw the warm, wooden walls of the cabin where I was staying in the North Woods.

105

But the sound, that dreadful sound, was still there.

I turned around and saw the old-fashioned clock hanging on the wall over my bed. It was ticking and tocking, ticking and tocking — its sound still tapping at my feverish brain.

Over the Hill

The scout troop had settled for the night in a valley between two large hills. A small creek ran through the valley near where they had set up camp. And the hills that crept up to the sky on both sides of it were covered with thick, dark trees. The two scout leaders, who were still teenagers, had never camped in this place before. But the trail leading into the valley had been easy to follow, and so they had led their group of ten younger scouts down to this spot.

The two leaders, Matt and John, were good scouts, but they weren't too concerned about the younger boys they had brought along on this camping trip. They had been stuck with the job after the senior scout leader had suddenly fallen ill. And so they let the younger boys take care of themselves while they sat around the fire and talked over their plans for what they would do after high school graduation.

One of the younger scouts, named Ben, came up and interrupted them. "Matt, what's on the other side of that hill?" he asked, pointing to the hill that lay on the other side of the valley from where they had come.

"No idea," Matt answered. "I've never been here before."

"Will we go there tomorrow?" Ben asked.

"No, we're turning right back around and going home," Matt said, "soon as you guys wake up."

"But what are we going to do tonight?" Ben asked, persistently. "This is boring, just sitting around."

Several of the other younger scouts had gathered behind Ben. They wanted to tell stories, or sing songs, or do anything but sit in their tents.

"Listen, Ben, if you're so bored, why don't you go over the hill?" John said, half as a joke. "You can take your flashlight and explore. How about it?"

"Okay, I'll do it," Ben answered. He looked a little scared, but he wasn't going to admit it to his friends.

Matt and John settled back to their conversation, not really paying any attention to what Ben was doing. The other boys watched from the campsite as Ben walked along the trail that led up the hill. They could see his flashlight beam climbing higher and higher up. It quavered a bit at the very top of the hill, and then disappeared as he went over the hill and down the other side.

The younger scouts sat and watched the spot on the top of the hill where Ben's light had disappeared. But it never came back. They sat and watched for twenty minutes. Then Leroy went to the camp fire to talk to the two leaders.

"Ben didn't come back," he said. "Somebody had better check on him."

Matt and John thought he was kidding. They didn't really want to be bothered, anyway.

"So, go find him," Matt said.

Leroy got his flashlight and set off on the trail up from the valley. The other scouts watched as the beam of his flashlight moved slowly up the hill. Leroy stopped several times and seemed to think about turning back. But then his flashlight beam traveled back upwards until, finally, it reached the top of the hill. It shone there for a few seconds, and then disappeared.

The boys waited for fifteen minutes. But Leroy's light never appeared again. This time, the rest of the eight boys went to the camp fire. They told Matt and John what had happened.

"Come on, they're just playing a game with you," John said. "Somebody always tries to pull something like this on a camping trip. You wait long enough, and they'll be sneaking back into camp to scare you."

The eight scouts went back to the place near their tents where they could stare up at the spot on the hill where they had last seen Ben's and Leroy's lights. They waited and waited, but the hill remained as dark as ever, a hulking shadow against the night sky.

Finally, the boys walked up to Matt and John again.

"We're going over the hill," one of them said, "to find Ben and Leroy."

"We'll watch you," Matt said, laughing. "And don't stay out too late."

The eight boys lined up with their flashlights and then began walking up the hill. From the camp fire in the valley, Matt and John could see the eight beams of their flashlights flickering and moving slowly up the trail. Every so often, the lights would stop, and then move on again. When the line of eight lights had almost reached the top of the hill, they suddenly began to come back down again, fast — as though the boys were running. But then they stopped, and slowly, like a funeral procession, began to move back upwards again. The lights reached the top and then went over the hill. And disappeared from sight.

Matt and John sat around the camp fire for another hour, talking and laughing. Then they began to get worried. Maybe this wasn't a prank after all. Maybe, they began to think, they should have taken better care of the younger scouts.

They got out their big lanterns, lit them, and then walked up the hill. On the way up, they searched every inch of the trail. When they reached the top, they looked over the other side of the hill.

Even in the moonlight, all they could see was blackness — nothing but blackness. They seemed to be looking into a big, dark hole that would swallow up anything that went into it. Matt and John called and called the younger boys' names. But no one answered. There wasn't any sound at all. In the morning, they sent out a search party. But no one ever found the ten scouts.

They had gone over the hill.

The Hitchhiker

One evening, at twilight, a man was driving along a lonely country road toward a town he'd never visited before. He was on a business trip, and he was watching the road signs carefully to see where he was going. The countryside around him was hilly and covered with pine trees. It was the kind of country that made him feel uneasy, because he'd grown up in the city. Like many city people, he found more to be afraid of in wide-open spaces that he did on crowded streets.

The shadows of the tall trees were growing longer and darker when he came to a fork where the road split in two different directions. The man peered at his map, but couldn't find this place anywhere on it. A feeling of panic began to grow in his mind as he looked down one of the desolate roads and then the other. It seemed that neither one led anywhere, and now the sky was turning a dark, inky blue.

Just then, a figure appeared only a few feet from his car door. It appeared so quickly that it seemed to come out of nowhere. The man quickly locked his car doors, and then watched nervously as the figure came closer. He saw that it was a woman, a young woman, and she seemed to be frightened, too. As she came closer to the car, he rolled down the window.

"Please, sir," she pleaded in a breathless voice. "Could you give me a ride?"

The man looked at her with sympathy. She was obviously harmless, he thought, and she needed help. Besides, he told himself, she would be able to direct him to the town he was looking for.

"Where can I take you?" he asked the young woman. "You look lost, too."

"Oh, no, I'm not lost," she said. "I live quite nearby. It's just that I need to be someplace soon, and I am too tired to walk."

The man told the young woman to get into the car, and that he would take her where she needed to go. After sitting down in the front seat, she directed him to take the left fork of the road and to drive on for about four miles.

Before starting off down the road, the man looked over at his passenger and noticed the paleness of her skin and the trembling of her hands. He wondered if she had just had a shock. But she didn't answer his questions about how she felt. She just asked him to please hurry. She had to be somewhere and had no time to waste.

The man began driving down the road to the left, glancing over at the young woman from time to time. The light was fading rapidly from the sky, but he could still see her clearly. As they drove on and it became darker, it seemed to him that her face was becoming thinner and thinner. Her eyes, when they met his, seemed to become darker and stared out from deep bony sockets in her face.

Suddenly, the man felt a tremor of fear pass through his body. He still had no idea where he was going. And this young woman was very strange.

"Will this road take me on to Wilsonville?" he asked, hoping that her answer would be yes.

"Oh, no," the young woman answered in a voice that suddenly sounded as thin and dry as old paper. "You'll have to turn around after you drop me off. Wilsonville is on the road that forks to the right."

Looking over at her in irritation, the man was shocked to see that her face looked almost like a skull, with bare teeth grinning at him. He quickly stared back at the road, telling himself that the light was bad and his imagination was getting the better of him.

A few minutes later, the young woman called out for him to stop. He braked on top of a hill and saw the white tombstones of a cemetery glowing in the moonlight on both sides of the road. Then he heard the car door open. And as he looked over to where his passenger had been, he saw a skeleton stepping away from the car into the cemetery.

The man didn't waste any time turning the car around and racing back down the road to the fork. No sooner had he pulled onto the road that went to the right than he saw the wreck of an automobile. It had exploded into flames and was burnt almost beyond recognition. A policeman was standing beside it, shaking his head as the man pulled up.

"Nothing could be done to save her," the policeman said. "She's among the dead now."

"I know," the man answered. "I just took her ghost to the graveyard."

The Blue Coffin

They say twins have a special way of communicating with each other — almost as if their two minds are one. This was true of the Jones twins from the minute they were born. If one started to cry as a baby, the other seemed to sense its pain and cry, too. As children, Mary and Maggie Jones learned to speak and read and add at the same time. Their two minds were like copies of each other and, often, they didn't need to speak in order to know what the other was thinking.

The two girls grew up to be identical in all ways — until they turned sixteen, that is. A month after their sixteenth birthday, Maggie suddenly became ill. It was a slow, creeping illness, the kind that no one even noticed at first. But the young girl lost weight, week after week, and soon her arms and legs were thin and spindly. Her face lost its rosy blush and took on a pale, grayish cast. Mary, meanwhile, stayed strong and healthy.

The parents took Maggie to doctor after doctor, but none of them could determine what illness she had. And none of them found a medicine or cure that could stop it. Sometimes, when she looked at her sick sister, Mary would suddenly be overcome by the same feeling of weakness that Maggie felt. She wanted to be able to give her own strength to Maggie, but not even she could help her sister.

After six months of getting weaker and weaker, Maggie stopped breathing one morning. Mary found her, lying quiet and still in her bed. To Mary, she didn't seem dead, just trapped in a very deep sleep. In fact, she seemed to still sense Maggie's feelings inside her own mind.

When their parents looked at Maggie, they began to cry and called the doctor. They knew she had to be dead, because she was not breathing and her pulse showed no sign of life. When the doctor came and examined the girl's limp, lifeless body, he confirmed their fears. Maggie had finally died of her mysterious illness.

Mary took the death worse than anyone. She sat by Maggie's bedside hour after hour, holding her hand. In fact, she refused to believe that her twin had died. Her parents had to lock her in her room when Maggie's body was taken away.

At the funeral, Mary looked down at Maggie in her favorite blue dress, lying on the blue satin of the coffin. Blue had been her favorite color and now she would be surrounded by it forever. The strange feeling that Maggie was still alive kept haunting Mary. But looking at the pale face with its grayish cast, she could see that was impossible. She felt as though part of herself had died, and she almost wished that she were lying beside Maggie in the coffin. Maggie looked at peace — while Mary felt tormented by her death.

They buried Maggie in the town graveyard that was only a block from the Joneses' house. That night, Mary fell asleep haunted by nightmares of being buried in that blue coffin under six feet of cold hard ground. Her parents sat beside Mary's bed until they knew that she was finally asleep. Then they went to their own bed to let sleep ease their grief.

Much later, in the middle of the night, they heard a terrible cry come from Mary's room. *Aaaaaaaaagggghhh!* She was screaming and screaming with terror. They rushed to her bedside, and saw her twisting and turning in her bed and clawing at the air above her.

"Let me out," she screamed. "Let me out!"

Her father shook Mary to wake her up. But then he realized that she was awake already, and she was still screaming and begging to be let out.

"Mary, Mary, what's the matter?" her mother asked.

"It's Maggie, she's alive," Mary sobbed. "She's alive in that blue coffin."

Her parents tried to comfort and calm Mary, but she would not be silenced.

"I can feel it," Mary said. "She wants out of that coffin. She can't breathe."

The parents didn't know what to do. They understood how close the twins had been. And the doctor had warned them that Mary might have a serious emotional reaction to Maggie's death.

"Mary, you must get those thoughts out of your mind," her father said. "Maggie is dead."

"No, she's not," Mary said. "She's trying to stay alive, but she can't breathe in that coffin."

Then Mary started to claw wildly at the air in front of her again.

Her mother began to sob, now half believing what Mary was saying. She began to beg her husband to go to the graveyard. Mary jumped up from her bed and got dressed.

"We have to save her, before it's too late," she cried.

The family rushed to the garage to get shovels and then drove through the night to the graveyard. With Mary in the lead, they ran to Maggie's grave and began to dig and shovel and dig and shovel the dirt that lay cold and heavy over Maggie's coffin. When they finally uncovered it, Mr.

Jones, with trembling hands, unlocked the coffin lid and lifted it up. By the light of the moon, they looked down into the blue coffin.

Maggie lay still in her coffin bed. She was finally dead. Her face was twisted in agony, as though she had fought and fought for breath and lost the battle. Her long, thin fingers were ragged and bloody from having scratched at the top of the coffin.

And the lid of the blue coffin, where she had been buried alive, was carved with deep marks from her frantic fingers.

The Bogey

"**H**ave they told you about the Bogey yet?"
Jeffrey felt his body tense. Kenny's whispering voice was so close to his ear that it sounded like a snake hissing. Kenny slept in the bunk next to his, and their heads were only inches apart.

"Be quiet," Jeffrey whispered back. "I'm trying to sleep."

"You don't know about him, do you?" Kenny sounded determined to talk, even though it was against the rules after lights out.

"So what if I don't?" Jeffrey said. "It sounds like a scary story."

"Listen, this is your first year at Camp Cypress," Kenny said. "You don't know half the stuff that goes on around here."

Jeffrey felt the hair stand up on the back of his neck. Kenny had just made him remember the creepy feeling he'd had when he first came to Camp Cypress, four days ago. It wasn't like the other camps he'd gone to. It was on the edge of a swamp. And it was more isolated and run down. Even his parents had looked a little nervous about leaving him.

"This place used to be an old private hideout," Kenny said in a low voice. "If you look around, you can find old coins and things."

Jeffrey lay in the darkness, breathing in and out nervously. He knew Kenny was going to tell him about the Bogey, even if he didn't want to hear it.

"About two hundred years ago," Kenny went on, "a pirate named Captain Bogey made his hideout here. He buried the treasure he'd stolen from hundreds of ships. But his first mate double crossed him. He shot Captain Bogey and stole the treasure. The captain slowly bled to death. But before he died, he vowed that his ghost would come back for revenge. And that's the Bogey. He still wanders through the swamp at night, carrying his knife. And he's still looking for revenge."

Jeffrey lay in the darkness, listening to his heart pound. He knew the story about the Bogey couldn't be true. But, still, he didn't like to think about it. The trees around Camp Cypress were so dark and thick. And, every night, the counselor of their cabin, Peter, made one of the campers go out in the middle of the night and get one of the charred logs from the camp bonfire — just to prove he wasn't afraid to do it. Of the boys in the cabin, four had already gone. That left only Kenny and himself for tonight.

As Jeffrey lay there in the dark, he heard Peter clear his throat from across the cabin. A nervous chill ran down his spine. That's what Peter always did just before he woke everybody up for the nightly test — the coward test, he called it.

"Ready to go tonight?" Kenny whispered in Jeffrey's ear with a snicker. "It's either you or me, and I already did it last year."

Jeffrey felt the nervous twinge in the pit of his stomach begin to spread throughout his body. He told himself that Kenny's story was just a joke. But the idea of the Bogey had begun to grow real in his mind.

"It's time for the test," Peter suddenly called out in his low voice that had an edge of meanness to it. Jeffrey heard the rest of the boys in the cabin groan and yawn. Everyone was getting used to Peter's trick of waking them up, but they still didn't like it. "Jeffrey, get up!" Peter's voice ordered. "You're taking a little walk tonight."

A rush of fear shot through Jeffrey's body, leaving his arms and legs feeling weak and heavy as stone. He struggled out of his bunk and pulled on a sweatshirt and his jeans.

"You know what you have to do, Jeffrey. You go through the swamp to where the big bonfire

123

was tonight. The trail is pretty dark this time of night, isn't it, guys?"

The voices of the four boys who had already done the test answered back with scary sounds.

"You pick up one of the charred logs from the bonfire, and then you come back here with it to prove you're not a coward."

Jeffrey swallowed hard and slipped his feet into his sneakers. He knew he couldn't refuse to go. That would brand him as a coward for the rest of the time he was at camp. As he headed for the door, Peter hissed in a low voice, "Don't let the Bogey get you."

Jeffrey stepped out onto the dark path that led away from the cabin to the bonfire site. He could hear the croaking of the frogs from the swamp. In the distance, he could see the other cabins of the camp. He wondered if any of the campers in the other cabins had to do the test. Or was it just Peter's sick idea?

Jeffrey squinted into the darkness ahead of him, trying to make out the trail through the dark trees. There was only a thin sliver of a moon to guide him, and he began to grope his way in the dark, feeling the trees along the sides of the narrow path.

A sudden sound made Jeffrey freeze in his tracks. It came again, a soft, scuffling noise from behind him. An animal, he told himself. He started down the path again, moving more quickly, trying to escape the sound that padded along behind him. But it kept following him, not sounding like an animal anymore. It sounded like . . . the Bogey.

The soggy earth of the trail suddenly came to an end at the bonfire, and Jeffrey rushed over to the cold embers. He felt around until he found one of the charred logs. And, then, he heard the soft thud of footsteps behind him. He clutched the log in his hands and jumped up, sensing the presence of something only inches away.

He whirled around and began to run back down the trail to the cabin. But the footsteps found him in the dark and followed closely behind, like evil shadows. Through the panic in his mind, Jeffrey thought about the sound of the footsteps. Their sound was muffled and soft. They came after him, slowly closing the distance between them, no matter how fast he ran.

"Don't let the Bogey get you." Peter's words raced through Jeffrey's mind with every breath he took. Jeffrey knew he was close to the cabin now, but the footsteps were close to him, too.

Then, with a sickening feeling, Jeffrey heard something slice through the air behind him. An intense pain cut through his back — once, twice — and he almost crumpled to the ground. But fear made him stagger on until, finally, he reached the cabin door. He stumbled into the cabin and dropped the log on the floor, panting like a wild animal that had escaped its predator.

Flashlights flicked on, piercing the darkness with beams of light. Jeffrey stood still, in shock, as the boys came out of their bunks.

"The Bogey," he whispered. "It chased me."

Peter laughed, and then Kenny. "There's no such thing as the Bogey, you fool," Peter said. "That was just a story — to scare you."

"The Bogey got me," Jeffrey gasped. Then his knees buckled and he dropped forward onto the floor in a faint. The other boys gathered around and shone their flashlights down onto his fallen body.

And then they saw it. On his back were two slashes in the form of an X — marked by Captain Bogey.

Night Creature

The family started off down the trail that led to the cabin they had rented deep in the woods. The cabin was deeper into the wilderness than they had ever been before. Not even the father was sure how far they had to walk from where they parked the car to the cabin. He had rented the cabin through the mail after answering an ad in a wilderness magazine.

"The woods are different around here," Meg said. "The trees are taller and thicker."

"And it's darker," David added. "Sort of creepy."

"Don't start scaring yourselves already," Mr. Jackson said. "We have a long way to walk yet. You'll feel more at ease once we find the cabin and get settled in."

"Remember, Rex is here to take care of us," Mrs. Jackson said. Rex wagged his tail at the mention of his name and bounded off ahead of them on the trail. He was a hunting dog and loved being in the woods.

The trail wound through the dense woods, farther and farther away from civilization. Mr. Jackson stopped several times to consult the map he had been sent through the mail. It was just a hand-drawn map, and he was beginning to worry about how accurate it was. They had already gone three times as far as he thought they would have to.

A loud howl echoed through the woods ahead of them. They all stopped, recognizing that it was Rex.

"He sounds upset," Meg said. "Maybe he doesn't like it here."

"He's probably smelled a fox or something," Mr. Jackson said, "and wishes he could catch it."

They all hurried on down the trail, feeling uneasy. Within a few minutes, they found Rex. He was standing in front of an old log cabin. The hair on his back was bristling as he prowled back and forth in front of the cabin, sniffing and whimpering.

"I guess this is it," David said, staring at the cabin.

"I don't like it any more than Rex does," Meg said. "It's not what I thought . . . it's scary."

The four of them stared in silence. Some of the logs had decayed over the years and, in places, a green fungus was growing over the wood. There were four small windows with glass panes, but they were scratched and blurred with age. The worst thing was the door. It was hanging loose from its hinges and standing wide open.

"Well, I guess I won't need the key they sent me in the mail," Mr. Jackson said, trying to sound lighthearted. "Let's go in."

But as the four moved toward the cabin, Rex loped over in front of the doorway and growled.

"He doesn't want us to go in," Meg said. "I think we should get out of here."

Mr. and Mrs. Jackson looked at each other with worried expressions. "It's too late to leave, kids," Mrs. Jackson said. "It'll be dark in an hour. We couldn't possibly make it back to the car on that trail."

Mr. Jackson stepped around Rex and went into the cabin, trying to ignore the dog's growling and whimpering. A few minutes later, he motioned for the rest of the family to come inside.

"It's not so bad," David said as he walked inside and looked around at the one-room cabin. "Except for the smell."

The smell was strange — a mixture of mold and animal scent. Mrs. Jackson went to the windows right away and pulled them open. "Well, at least there are cots for us to sleep on," she said. "After all, we just have to make it through the night. We can leave in the morning if we want to, can't we?" She gave her husband a pleading look.

"We'll see how it goes tonight," he said.

Everyone got busy unpacking their backpacks. The horrible smell seemed to lessen as the wind from the woods blew through the cabin. By the time they all had eaten a meal cooked on their camp stove outside, everyone was in better spirits.

"I wish Rex would stop prowling around and whimpering," Meg said. "He makes me nervous. Every time I start to feel relaxed here, I see him sniffing around like something is wrong."

"Don't worry," her father said, "that's just the hunting dog in him. He'll settle down."

But Mr. Jackson was wrong. Even after they had all gotten into their sleeping bags for the night and closed and locked the cabin door, Rex didn't settle down. He kept prowling around the cabin, whimpering and letting out low growls.

Finally, the family fell asleep from exhaustion. But deep in the night, they woke up.

"What was that?" David whispered. They all sat up in the darkness and waited.

A weird cry came through the woods. It didn't sound like any animal they'd ever heard before. The cry was part whine, part moan, and part blood-curdling howl.

130

"Hurry, shut the windows," Mrs. Jackson said frantically. Everyone sensed the same fear. They didn't know what the sound was coming from. But they didn't want the creature that was making it inside the cabin.

The cry shrieked through the dark woods again as they scrambled out of their sleeping bags and rushed toward the windows. Rex let out a loud bark and then continued to growl, pacing closer and closer to one of the windows.

"Hurry, shut that window!" Mrs. Jackson called to David. But he was too late. Rex took a running leap and jumped through the last open window into the night, barking and growling.

The four of them stood in the dark, trembling. No one made a move to shut the window again. They all wondered what would happen to Rex if he found that creature in the woods.

They waited and worried in the dark. The woods echoed with the creature's weird cry and Rex's snarls and barks. When the dog hadn't come back after two hours, Mr. Jackson finally shut the window. Then they all fell into an exhausted sleep.

The next morning, everyone was awakened by the sound of scratching and whimpering at the door. The sunlight was pouring into the cabin, and the horror of the night before seemed to have all been a nightmare.

But when they opened the door, they saw that Rex had changed. His eyes were glazed over with fear. He walked hunched down with his head hanging. And his coat was white . . . pure white.

It had been black — until he met the creature of the night.

The Thing in
the Back Seat

It was the night after Karen turned sixteen. She had begged her father to let her get a car for her birthday. After hearing her ask again and again, he finally gave in and said yes. They drove to the used car lot right after dinner. Karen had gotten her driver's license just that afternoon, and she drove her father's large sedan cautiously down the road.

They had agreed that the car should not cost much, and that it would not be too sporty or fast. Secretly, Karen hoped that she might find a bright red car, maybe even a convertible, and convince her father to buy it. But she was willing to settle on anything he agreed to buy. After all, what she really wanted was a set of wheels to give her freedom. Freedom to drive away from home and speed down the road with the wind blowing through her hair.

As soon as they drove up to the lot and parked, Karen jumped out of the car and started to walk up and down the rows of used cars. She couldn't help but feel disappointed. Most of them were family cars with four doors, dull colors, and no personality. She couldn't imagine herself behind the wheel of one of these cars, but she kept trying to tell herself that any car was better than no car.

The salesman came up to her father and started to ask questions. A crooked smile came over his face as he listened to what they were looking for. Then, with a flourish of his arm, he waved them toward a brown sedan that had orange upholstery with plastic seat covers. Karen cringed and tried to pull her father away from the car, but he seemed intent on listening to the salesman's pitch. She crept away from the car, deciding that she wouldn't be caught dead in it.

She backed into a red convertible that had a price tag that was ten times what her father had promised to pay. Still, she couldn't resist slipping into the driver's seat. The minute she gripped the wheel in her hands, she knew it was the car she wanted. Then she looked through the windshield and saw her father's frowning face coming toward her. Quickly, she jumped out of the car and walked toward him, not whispering a word about the convertible.

For another hour, they followed the salesman around the lot as he showed them one car after another. One was too expensive, another too ugly, the next too run-down. Karen began to despair of ever getting a car. She walked away from her father and the salesman and started to wander toward the back of the lot. It was the only place she hadn't looked yet, and she was feeling desperate.

Then, like a miracle, she saw the car. It was dark red — something like the color of dried blood — but just bright enough to look sporty. It wasn't a convertible, but it was sleek and low and had the kind of style she liked. And, best of all, the price was just below what she and her father had agreed on. Karen slipped behind the wheel and settled into the leather bucket seat. The minute she put her hands on the steering wheel, she knew it was the car she had to have.

Suddenly, she saw the salesman walking briskly across the lot toward her, shaking his head.

"No, no, no," he said emphatically. "You do not want that car, young lady."

"I'm afraid you're wrong," she answered just as firmly. "It's exactly the car I want."

Her father came up then and saw her sitting behind the wheel. She noticed the smile that spread across his face when he saw the price tag on the car.

"Well, well, why haven't you shown us this beauty before?" he asked the salesman.

"Listen, everyone who buys this car brings it back," the salesman said. "Trust me."

Karen met her father's eyes. She knew that something about the car had caught his fancy as well. Right away, she went to work convincing him that she should have it. Her father opened up the hood and looked at the engine. As far as he could tell, the car was in perfect shape.

"I think we'll buy it," he told the salesman. "I can write out a check tonight."

"You're just wasting your time," the salesman said. "Everybody who buys this car brings it back."

Karen and her father didn't pay any attention to what he said. They paid for the car and Karen drove it off the lot. All the way home, she kept the windows down so the wind could blow through her hair. She felt free, even though the wind was cold and stung her cheeks.

The next day after school, Karen grabbed her set of car keys and ran out to the car. She jumped inside and took off on a road that led out of town. It was a brisk autumn day and when she rolled down the windows, she became chilled by the cool breeze. Reluctantly, she rolled the windows up again and drove on.

Before long, she began to notice a strange smell. It seemed to be coming from the back seat. The longer she drove on smelling that smell, the sicker she felt. It was a sweet rotting smell, a disgusting aroma that reminded her of graveyards. Karen suddenly didn't feel free anymore and quickly turned the car around to go home.

The next day, the same thing happened. She had to roll the windows up because the weather was so cool. When she did, the whole car began to reek with the rotting smell from the back seat. This time, Karen decided to keep driving, even though the smell bothered her. As she went on, the smell got worse and worse and almost seemed to be alive in the back seat. She glanced up at the rearview mirror, and there, staring back at her, were two evil eyes. Karen screamed and whirled around to look in the back seat. But nothing was there — just the horrible smell.

The next day, Karen decided she wouldn't take a drive in her new car. Then her mother asked her to go on an errand to the next town, and Karen was too embarrassed to admit that she was afraid of the car. So she climbed behind the wheel, rolled down the windows even though it was freezing cold out, and started to drive.

For several miles, it seemed that nothing was wrong with the car at all. Karen almost started to feel the sense of freedom again that she'd first experienced when she sat behind the wheel. Then, when she was all alone on the country road, the smell began. It grew and grew until it filled up the back seat. Then Karen took courage and looked into her rearview mirror. The evil eyes were there again, staring at her. They narrowed as she met their gaze. Karen started to scream. Just as she did, a hand reached from the back seat and grabbed her shoulder. She whirled around. But there was nothing there!

Karen slammed down on the brake, and the car screeched to a stop. As she threw open the door, she felt the hand from the back seat grab at her neck. She looked up into the rearview mirror, and the eyes were there, leering at her. With all her strength, she pulled loose and jumped from the car. She ran all the way home, trying to escape the thing in the back seat.

The next day, Karen and her father took the car back to the lot. The salesman shook his head when he saw them. By evening, the car was back in its place at the rear of the lot.

The thing in the back seat was there, too . . . waiting.

Night Bite

Nancy dreaded the overnight camp-out more than anything else. The idea of spending the night in a sleeping bag in the middle of the woods made her sick with fear. She wanted to run away from camp and go home. But she couldn't do that, of course. Her parents expected her to love camp and the great outdoors. If they only knew.

Now here she was, on the camp-out, sitting around the fire listening to the scary stories everyone liked to tell. Stories about ghosts, vampires, and weird creatures that lived in the woods. She hated the stories. But at least they kept her from having to crawl into her damp sleeping bag on the hard ground. Nancy hadn't told anyone why she hated these overnights in the woods so much. It was her secret, and she was afraid to let the other campers know. They were sure to use it against her. You see, she had a terrible fear of insects.

Once, in the cabin, a daddy longlegs spider had

crawled across her bunk. She had watched its long, thin legs pick their way across her sheet, right over her stomach. She had been too terrified to touch it, or brush it away. And she was afraid to scream because the other girls would find out she was scared. She had just lain there, stiff with fright, while the spider pranced across her body. Now, she was in the middle of the woods with no roof, walls, or floor to protect her.

The flames of the camp fire were burning low, and the head counselor finally told everyone it was time to go to sleep. Nancy wished she felt more tired, but her mind was racing . . . imagining the insects that must be creeping around in the woods: spiders, beetles, ticks, every kind of horrible six-legged jumping or squirming creature.

All the other girls had arranged their sleeping bags together so they could talk and tell stories. As usual, Nancy hadn't been included. She had dragged her sleeping bag near everyone else's. But she was still closer to the trees that surrounded the campsite than anyone else. She wanted to complain and ask to be closer to the fire, which would surely keep away any insects coming near it. But she knew it was no use. The counselor didn't have pity on anyone who was weak. And the other girls would only make fun of her.

Nancy placed the head of her sleeping bag as

far away from the trees as possible and then carefully unzipped it, checking every inch for a hidden insect. When she was satisfied that it was clean, she slipped her body inside and zipped up the bag all the way, even though the night was hot and sticky. She lay there, staring up at the moon, thinking about all the insects that might be crawling across the ground toward her. In her mind, they became like an army — spiders with long spindly legs, ants with bulging eyes, beetles with hard bodies, millipedes with thousands of creepy legs. After what seemed like hours of this waking nightmare, Nancy finally fell asleep.

Her own scream woke her up. At first she thought she was screaming in a nightmare — the worst nightmare she'd ever had. She was dreaming that a huge insect was covering her face and biting her. But then she realized that the scream was real and some horrible thing *was* on her face, biting her. In a panic, she twisted out of her sleeping bag and frantically brushed off her face.

It was early dawn, and her scream had woken up the other girls. They were staring at her with sleepy, scared eyes. Nancy saw that all their eyes were fixed on her right cheek. It was stinging. She quickly raised her hand to the spot and felt a large bump that itched and was hot. It was a bite. An insect bite.

Nancy screamed again and started to brush off

141

all over her body. She was terrified that the insect was still on her. The other girls started to laugh at her and point at the red spot on her face. Finally, the counselor forced her to calm down and to stop trying to brush away the insect that was no longer there. But, all the rest of the day, Nancy's hand kept creeping back up to her face to feel the horrible, stinging spot.

That night, all the campers went back to the cabin to sleep. But Nancy didn't sleep — not for a long time. She had looked at the bite in the mirror in the camp washroom. It was big and swollen and red. All she could think about was the insect that had bitten her. In her mind it grew bigger and bigger and more frightful-looking. All night long, she kept brushing that insect off her face until just before dawn when she fell asleep.

The next day she went to see the camp nurse about the bite. The nurse examined it carefully and said it wasn't a tick bite. That's all she seemed to care about. She told Nancy to leave the bite alone and it would go away.

But the bite didn't go away. Every day it got redder and redder and bigger and bigger. Everyone at camp stared at it and laughed. And every time they stared, Nancy felt that insect crawling across her face and biting her.

Finally, one evening, Nancy went to the washroom and stood in front of the mirror, staring at the horrible red spot on her face. It was swollen bigger than ever and hurt her cheek. She reached down to the sink and splashed hot water on the spot. Then, all of a sudden, it burst open.

And, while she stared at herself in the mirror, Nancy saw ten little black spiders crawl out of their eggs and scurry across her face.

The Red Bandanna

It was quiet hour. I lay on my bottom bunk thinking about the seven other girls I would be sharing this cabin with for the next two weeks. This morning we had been strangers. But, already, we knew a lot about each other. We knew who was the greediest for food in the dining hall. We knew who was afraid of spiders. And we all knew who would be the outsider in the cabin — Charlotte, the girl in the top bunk above me. Charlotte, with her red bandanna around her neck.

I could hear Charlotte's breathing right now. She must be asleep, I thought, because her breath was coming in long, raspy sounds. I started to grit my teeth together as I listened to that sound, over and over again. I couldn't believe that I had to sleep in the bunk under Charlotte for two whole weeks. It was enough to make me want to go home.

144

Just then, I heard Liz clear her throat across the cabin from me. I glanced over and caught her eye. She pointed up to Charlotte and then made a choking motion with her hands. We both started to giggle until Laura, our counselor, jumped out of her bunk and came over to give us a mean stare. I went back to reading my book of ghost stories and tried to ignore Charlotte's breathing until quiet hour finally ended.

The counselor had to shake Charlotte awake to get ready for our swimming lesson. We all got into our suits, grabbed our towels, and waited impatiently for Charlotte to join us outside the cabin. When she finally came out, we stared at her in disbelief. She had on her swimming suit, but the red bandanna was still around her neck.

"Charlotte," Laura said, "take your bandanna off and leave it in the cabin. Then we can all get going."

"No," Charlotte said with a determined edge to her voice. "I can't."

Liz and I stared at each other and made big eyes. Charlotte was even stranger than we thought.

Laura opened her mouth to start to say something, but she must have decided not to argue with Charlotte in front of the rest of us. We all headed down to the lake, glancing every once in a while at the red bandanna around Charlotte's neck.

The cold water of the lake felt good because it was a hot and sticky day. We all had races swimming back and forth between the dock and a diving platform about fifty yards out into the lake — all of us but Charlotte. She got wet once, but then just sat on the dock shivering and twisting the ends of the red bandanna around her fingers.

When we went back to the cabin to change, Charlotte still kept on the red bandanna, even though it was wet and soppy. We all started to whisper among ourselves about why she kept it on. Did she have some horrible scar underneath it? Was it some kind of weird security blanket? Liz even came right out and asked Charlotte why she didn't take it off. Charlotte just said, "I can't."

Charlotte became the joke of our cabin. What we did to her wasn't nice, but you know how it is at camp. Somebody always gets picked on. We short-sheeted her bunk. We hid a frog in her duffel bag. We made fun of her raspy breathing at night, imitating her and then laughing until even Laura joined in.

But after three nights of listening to that horrible, raspy breathing, I was at the end of my wits. It was our fourth night in the cabin. The temperature had soared into the high nineties during the day, and the night air was still hot and sticky. I hadn't been able to get a decent night's sleep ever since I'd come, and now I was tossing and turning, listening to Charlotte's breathing.

"Maybe it's that bandanna," I whispered to Liz. "Maybe that's why she makes so much noise when she sleeps."

"Why doesn't she just take it off?" Liz said.

"Why don't we?" I said. "Maybe we could get some peace and quiet then."

"Good idea," I heard Kate say from another bunk.

"Let's see what's underneath it," Mary added in the dark.

Liz started to giggle and said, "Let's do it."

We knew Laura had to be awake, but she didn't let on. She probably wanted to stop Charlotte's noisy breathing as much as we did. And I'll bet she was as curious as we were about what was under the red bandanna.

Liz searched around in the dark for her little flashlight and then handed it to me. Everybody sat up in their bunks to watch as Liz climbed up the side of Charlotte's bunk. I got out of mine and held the flashlight for Liz as she reached over Charlotte's head and started to untie the red bandanna.

I could see that her hands were shaking as she struggled to loosen the knot that held the bandanna tight around Charlotte's neck. I thought

147

that Charlotte would wake up for sure. But her heavy, raspy breathing just went on and on.

Liz finally undid the first knot of the bandanna. Charlotte's breathing suddenly became louder and raspier. It sounded scary. I noticed that the light was quivering now because my hands had started to shake.

But Liz kept on working at the last knot of the bandanna. Everyone had gathered close around to watch. Finally, Liz worked the knot loose, and the red bandanna fell away from around Charlotte's neck. There was a sharp, choking sound in Charlotte's throat, and her eyes suddenly flew open.

Then her head slowly began to roll off her neck. And it fell right off the top bunk onto the floor.

STILL MORE

Contents

The Club

Have you ever moved to a new town where you had no friends? If you have, you'll know what it was like for Julio. He felt lonely. Bored. Desperate. He was so desperate that he almost joined the club. . . .

Julio was going into the last grade of middle school the year he moved to Los Padres. It was a tough time to move. Everyone was trying to be cool, and nobody seemed to have room in their group of friends for a quiet new kid. Julio spent a lot of time walking the streets of the town, hoping someone might start up a conversation. Nobody ever did.

Home wasn't so great, either. Julio's father worked late hours in a town that was over an hour away. His mother was so busy fixing up the house that she didn't have time for him. His older sister holed up in her room and listened to music. Julio started taking longer and longer walks, even after it got dark.

One night, he heard someone call out to him, someone who sounded friendly. It happened just as he was passing by the old town cemetery.

"Hey, we saw you walking by here last night. Who are you?"

Julio stopped short and looked into the cemetery. He saw three guys about his age sitting on a group of tombstones.

Julio walked closer to the low cemetery wall to get a better look at the three boys.

"I'm Julio Sanchez. I just moved into town last month."

"Hi, I'm Jim," said the boy who had called out. "And these are my friends Wiley and Tom. Why don't you come in and talk for a while?"

Julio looked into the dark graveyard and then turned around to look up and down the street. It didn't seem safe to walk into a cemetery at night. But these guys seemed friendly. And he was really lonely. Without hesitating anymore, Julio swung his legs over the low stone wall and walked into the graveyard.

"You can sit there," Jim said, pointing to a tombstone that faced his. "We were just having a meeting of our club."

"We meet here just about every night," Wiley added.

"Well, I don't want to interrupt or anything," Julio said.

"No problem," Tom said. "Hang around for a while."

"Okay, thanks," Julio said. His eyes were slowly adjusting to the dim light in the graveyard, and he tried to make out the faces of the three boys sitting in front of him. He could see their eyes clearly, but it was too dark to tell what they really looked like. Probably he'd never recognize them if he saw them on the street in the daylight.

"So, how do you like living here?" Jim asked.

"Kind of boring," Julio said. "I haven't gotten to know many kids yet."

"I remember what that was like," Wiley said. "Life can be a real drag."

"We three are lucky we got together," Tom added. "It gets pretty lonely hanging around by yourself."

"So does your club have a name or anything?" Julio asked.

"We call it the Cemetery Club," Jim said with a laugh. "Not very original, huh?"

"Sounds kind of original to me," Julio said. "Why do you meet here?" He felt really relaxed with these three guys, but it still seemed kind of weird that they were all hanging out in a grave-yard.

"It's close to home," Wiley said. "Anyway,

what's wrong with it? Does this place give you the creeps or something?"

Julio looked around at the rows of tombstones sitting like little white houses in the cemetery. He'd never thought of cemeteries as being anything else but creepy. But being here with friends made it feel different. Quiet . . . and peaceful.

"No, it doesn't really bother me," Julio said, trying to sound brave. "But aren't there bats and other scary things around?" He was almost going to mention ghosts, but he was afraid the three friends would laugh at him.

"Hey, the things in a graveyard aren't any more scary than what you'll meet out on the street," Jim said. "Ever think of it that way?"

"No," Julio answered with a nervous laugh. "And you guys are a lot nicer than anyone I've met on the street."

"Well, maybe you can join our club," Tom said. "If you really want to, that is."

"Yeah, I think I might like to do that," Julio answered. "When's the next meeting?"

"Tomorrow night, same time, same place," Jim said. "But you can't be a real member of the club without going through . . . like an initiation. And you have to be really sure you want to join."

"Take twenty-four hours to think it over," Wiley

said. "And come back tomorrow night to give us your answer."

The three boys had suddenly gotten up from their tombstones and were fading back into the dark shadows of the cemetery.

"Okay, I will," Julio called after them. "Tomorrow night. Same time. Same place."

He didn't know if Jim, Wiley, and Tom heard him, because they had disappeared into the cemetery. Julio felt the cold marble of the tombstone underneath him, and suddenly a chill shot through his body. He jumped up and ran over to the stone wall of the cemetery. He crossed it with a leap and ran down the street toward home. All the way there, he thought about the club.

The next night, Julio walked toward the cemetery with a smile on his face. He'd made up his mind. He was going to join. Jim, Wiley, and Tom were the only kids in the new town who'd paid any attention to him so far. And they'd probably be in the middle school when classes started again in a few weeks. It would be great to have three friends you knew you could count on.

Julio came up to the place in the cemetery where he had met the boys the night before. He peered into the shadowy graveyard, but no one was there. Then it suddenly hit him. They had just

159

been making fun of him last night. There really wasn't any club. And the next time he saw Jim, Wiley, and Tom, they would tease him for believing them.

Julio turned away from the cemetery and looked up the lonely street toward home.

"Hey, Julio, you came," Jim's voice called out from the cemetery.

Julio whirled around and saw the three boys sitting on the same tombstones. He couldn't believe that they hadn't been there a minute ago.

"We thought you might not show," Wiley said. "Not everybody is ready to be a member of the Cemetery Club."

"Well, I am," Julio said, jumping over the fence. He walked over and sat down on the same tombstone he had sat on the night before.

"Okay, then, let's start walking," Jim said.

The three boys were off their tombstones and moving through the cemetery before Julio could ask any questions. He caught up with them as they slipped between the graves and climbed a steep hill that rose to the top of the graveyard.

Julio struggled along behind them, barely keeping up. Even though they didn't seem to have any trouble, he was getting caught by bramble bushes and tripping over low tombstones. And the hill was much steeper than it had looked from the street. By the time he reached the top, where Jim,

Wiley, and Tom were waiting, Julio was short of breath and sweating ... from exhaustion and from a sense of fear that had been slowly creeping over him.

"Okay, this is the place," Jim said, pointing down into the darkness in front of them.

Julio suddenly realized where they were standing. The steep hill in the cemetery was really one side of a high cliff that overlooked the town. For a minute, a wave of dizziness came over him. He grabbed out for Jim's arm, but he just caught air.

"Are you all right?" Wiley asked. "You still want to go through with it, don't you?"

"We really want you to be part of the club," Tom said.

"It's tough at first," Jim added. "But then you're with friends ... forever."

Julio gulped. Suddenly he was afraid. But he didn't want to chicken out. This really was the only chance he had to make friends.

"So what do I do?" he asked.

"Jump," Jim said.

A pang of fear shot through Julio's body. "I can't do that," he said.

"Do you want to be a member of the club or not?" Jim asked.

Julio looked at the three boys in the moonlight. He wasn't so sure anymore. They looked different now. And scarier. Their eyes were sunken into their faces. And their bodies seemed so thin — almost like skeletons.

A shudder of fear traveled through Julio's body. Suddenly, he understood.

"You said you wanted to join the club," Wiley said.

"And to be a ghost," Jim added, "first you have to die."

"N-o-o-o-o!" Julio screamed as he ran past them and back down the hill. He ran and ran until he was out of the graveyard.

He stopped only once to look back. There, in the cemetery, he saw Jim, Wiley, and Tom sitting on their tombstones. Then, just like ghosts, they disappeared.

Audrey

In the beginning, I was as mean to Audrey as the rest of the kids were. She was new in school, but it wasn't just her newness that made her different. Audrey was so different that she might as well have been from another planet.

Her parents made her wear skirts or dresses all the time. And they were so long and dowdy that Audrey looked like an old woman. Her face was different, too. No makeup, of course. But it was more than just that. Her eyes were deep brown, with darkish circles under them. Her mouth was always set in a thin line, and she never laughed. Her brown hair hung to her shoulders without a curl or curve. And she wore a corny necklace all the time, a locket in the shape of a heart with an initial A carved on it. That was Audrey.

There was one more thing about Audrey. She wanted to be my friend more than anything in the world.

"Go away!" my friends would say to Audrey when she first started following us around. They all knew that Audrey wanted to be with me. It was obvious because she always tried to sit beside me in class, and she always volunteered to be my partner for projects. I was kind of embarrassed by her attention. I wondered what I had done to make her so loyal to me.

After a while, Audrey got the hint when my friends closed her out of our circle. But I think she knew that I always understood how she felt. Because I couldn't be mean to her. Somewhere inside me, I knew what Audrey was feeling. It was weird in a way . . . almost as though we were twins separated at birth, but I was the pretty, popular one and she was the dull, ordinary one.

By the end of October, Audrey had pretty much stopped following me around. My friends all made jokes about having gotten rid of her. So they were really surprised when I made out the list for my annual Halloween party. Audrey was on it.

"Are you crazy?" my best friend, Amanda, said. "Finally you get rid of that parasite, and now you invite her to your party. It's going to start all over again — she'll try to sit with you at lunch, she'll call you after school, she'll be pestering all of us."

"It's not going to hurt anybody if Audrey is at the party," I said, feeling a little embarrassed.

"There's going to be forty people there. Audrey won't get in anybody's way."

"You just feel guilty," my friend Diane accused me. "But if you invite her to the party, she'll just start wanting to be with you again. Then we'll all have to be mean again, and you'll end up feeling even more guilty."

I didn't listen to what any of them said. The next day at school I handed Audrey her invitation to the party. I watched as she opened it up and read it. Then she looked up at me and smiled the most beautiful smile I had ever seen. It lit up her whole face.

"Thank you," Audrey said. "I'll be there, no matter what."

"Great," I said. "It's a costume party, you know. Starts at seven-thirty . . ." I sort of trailed off because I didn't know what else to say. I almost apologized for how my friends had treated her. But Audrey looked so happy that finally I just smiled back and then walked away.

On Halloween night I was so nervous that I just about jumped out of my skin when my brother dangled a rubber spider in my face. I loved giving parties, but I worried about every little thing — the decorations, the food, how my parents would act — until the first guest arrived. Then I relaxed and enjoyed myself.

The first person to arrive that night was Amanda. She was dressed as a hippie from the sixties, and even I didn't recognize her right away.

"Far out," I said, looking at her costume. Then the doorbell rang again, and a flood of people started to arrive.

Kara came as a flapper, Emily was a cat, Gwen was Peter Pan, Jim was a mummy, Andrew was Frankenstein. Within fifteen minutes, the house was filled with my friends all in funny and strange costumes, all shrieking with laughter and having a great time.

I rushed around, trying to make sure that everybody had enough to eat. But in the back of my mind, something was nagging at me. Where was Audrey? She had sounded so happy about getting an invitation. And for some strange reason, I was really looking forward to seeing her. Had her parents stopped her from coming?

We started to bob for apples, then played a couple of games. I almost forgot about Audrey until the doorbell rang at 8:30. I rushed over to it, wondering if it might be her or some trick-or-treaters. I opened the door, and for a second, my heart stopped beating.

Audrey stood on the doorstep, staring straight into my eyes. She didn't have a costume on. In fact, she had on one of her old school dresses. The locket was hanging around her neck, as always. But there was something more frightening about Audrey than anyone else in a strange costume. It was her face. Her skin was even paler than usual. Her eyes were sunken in, and they had a haunted look that was almost desperate.

"Audrey, come in," I said. "Are you all right? You look . . . well, tired or scared."

"I wanted to come to your party so much," Audrey said. "I'd do anything to be here tonight."

I reached out to take her hand to lead her into the room, but it was so cold that I dropped it.

"I'll get you some warm cider," I said. "Sit down for a while, if you want."

Audrey curved her lips a little into a smile. Then she went and sat in a big chair in the corner of the living room. She looked happy there, all alone. I brought her the cider and then said I'd have to look in on the party.

"Thank you for asking me tonight," she said. "I'll never forget it."

Right then I got the same weird feeling that Audrey and I were twins — that we were sharing the same thoughts. But this time, I felt as though I was in another world — far, far away from the party going on around me. A chill shot through my body, and I started to shake all over. I looked into Audrey's eyes, and suddenly I got really scared.

167

"Hey, you're missing the party!" Amanda's voice shouted in my ear. "We need you to get more food."

I snapped out of whatever had come over me. It had been scary, and this time I couldn't wait to get away from Audrey.

"She looks like a ghost, even without a costume," Amanda whispered in my ear. "What were you thinking, asking her here tonight?"

"I don't know," I said shakily.

"Well, we all told you not to ask her. Now she'll always be haunting you."

Throughout the night, while I was having a good time with everyone else, I'd look over to that chair in the corner and see Audrey. She'd be looking back at me with her deep, dark eyes, and then she'd smile. It seemed as the night went on that her smile became weaker and weaker. Then, at about 11:45, I saw her get up from her chair and start to walk to the door.

She seemed to know that I would follow her.

"Thanks for coming, Audrey," I said as we reached the door. "I'm sorry I couldn't spend more time with you."

"You asked me to come," she answered. "That's what's important. And I'll always be your friend. Always."

A big lump rose in my throat. I didn't know what to say to her. I was touched, but I was scared, too. Then she reached around her neck and undid the clasp to her locket. A minute later, I felt her cold, cold fingers around my neck. She fastened the clasp of the locket at the back of my neck and then looked down at the gold heart with the A on it hanging below my face.

"Never take it off," she said. "So you'll never forget me."

Before I could say anything, Audrey was out the door. It was almost as though she had disappeared. I realized that my knees were shaking and my heart was pounding. I turned around and walked back to the party. But I didn't have any more fun that night. I couldn't forget Audrey.

The next morning in school, Ms. Sloan, our homeroom teacher, told us the news. Audrey wouldn't be with the class anymore. She was killed by a hit-and-run driver the night before at 7:30. Her parents had refused to let her go to a Halloween party. She had run away and tried to get there by herself.

Everyone in the class who had been at my party gasped and turned to stare at me. I reached up and clutched the gold locket around my neck.

And I knew Audrey was right. I would never forget her.

The Ring

An icy shiver cut down Benjamin's spine. He had two miles to walk through the cold February air. And the storm from the night before had made the sides of the road soggy and dangerous. Worst of all, he was late.

In half an hour, he was due at Ellen's house. They were making plans for their wedding, and she had warned him not to be late. Her parents were already disappointed by her choice of a future husband. Benjamin was so poor that he hadn't been able to buy Ellen a diamond engagement ring. On her left hand she wore only the narrow gold band that his grandmother had willed him. It would have to do as a wedding band as well.

Benjamin checked his watch and saw that he was getting later by the minute. As he came up to the old town graveyard, he remembered that there was a shortcut through it to Ellen's side of town. He looked at the narrow stone path that wound through the cemetery. It looked no worse than the muddy sides of the road that he had been walking on. And no cars would come along to splash him.

Benjamin gazed up at the darkening sky, filled with heavy gray clouds. Bare tree branches lashed above him, as though they were angry at the weather. He pulled his coat collar up tighter around his neck and struck off down the path.

In the middle of the cemetery, there was a hollow that Benjamin had forgotten about. As he looked down into it, he saw that the path was covered with water there. There was no time to turn back, he decided. He'd have to push on and walk around the hollow through the old tombstones. At least Ellen's house lay directly on the other side of the graveyard where the path led.

Benjamin looked up at the sky again, his face etched with worry. He didn't like being in the cemetery at night. But if he hurried, he would make it out just before the light faded completely. He began to thread his way through the old tombstones, noticing that many were over a hundred years old. The storm had knocked some of them over, and the ground was even soggier than the sides of the road.

Benjamin looked up to see how far he had to circle around before he made it back to the path.

When he looked down again, he saw something at his feet that made his breath choke back in his throat.

The storm had washed away the dirt from one of the gravesites, and lying on the cold wet ground in front of him was a skeleton. The tombstone at its head had fallen over and sunk into the muddy ground. Benjamin could see the rotted remains of a wooden coffin underneath the skeleton. But what caught his eye in the dim twilight was the ring. It sparkled even in the gloom of this stormy night.

For a few minutes, Benjamin froze in his footsteps. The sight of the skeleton had frightened him. But he couldn't take his eyes off the ring. It was the sort of ring he knew Ellen had dreamed about. Fate seemed to have brought him to this spot. And the skeleton's hand seemed to be reaching out to him, offering him the ring.

On trembling knees, Benjamin reached down and felt the tips of the skeleton's fingers. Immediately, he shrank back from their cold touch. But the ring beckoned him. He couldn't turn his eyes away from it.

Again, Benjamin reached out for the bony hand. This time, he forced himself to pick it up. Then he reached out to slip off the ring. Suddenly, the skeleton's fingers seemed to curl down and dig into his hand. Benjamin jumped back with a scream and dropped the hand. He looked away from the skeleton to the inky blue sky. What was he doing? He shouldn't waste any more time. He should just get out of the cemetery.

But the ring drew him toward it like an obsession. He wanted it for Ellen. Once more, he bent down and picked up the hand. It felt freezing cold, but Benjamin didn't let himself think. He jerked the ring off the bony finger, thrust it in his pocket, and then started to run. By the time he reached the edge of the graveyard, his heart was pounding like a frightened animal's. He wasn't sure if he was happy that he had taken the ring or not.

His feelings changed a half hour later when he slipped the ring onto Ellen's finger. She looked at him with glowing eyes and seemed to believe his story that he had been saving for the ring and only now could afford it. Even her parents treated him better. They all sat together making final plans for the wedding. It would take place the following week. And Ellen would be wearing her diamond engagement ring to the altar.

The night before the wedding, Ellen kissed Benjamin good night at her door, thanking him again for the beautiful ring. All week she had been wearing it proudly, showing it off to her friends and relatives. But she had told no one about the dreams she was having. The dreams troubled her sleep and gave her headaches during the day. She decided that they were just part of the nervousness she felt about the wedding. But the dreams were disturbing. And terrifying.

Ellen went up to her bedroom and got ready for her last night alone. She noticed that, as on other nights, the ring seemed to get colder on her finger as it got later. Shivering, she put on her warmest nightgown and crawled under the thick blankets on her bed. For a long time, she tossed and turned. She wanted to go to sleep, but she was afraid of the dreams. She didn't want them to come again.

And the ring. It was getting so cold on her finger again. Just like the other nights. The coldness stole through her bones and drained away her body's warmth. The diamond itself felt like a piece of ice. Ellen wanted to slip the ring off her finger, but she knew that was wrong. It might mean bad luck for her marriage the next day.

Ellen lay in bed shivering. Suddenly she heard a sound that made her freeze into stillness. It was the clicking sound of bones in her room. Her beautiful ring seemed to burn her flesh with its coldness.

Then a voice cut through the darkness.

"I've come for my ring."

"No," Ellen whimpered. "I don't have your ring, only mine."

The bones rattled nearer to her bed. Ellen felt a freezing draft of air sweep over her.

"I've come for my ring," the voice said again.

Ellen tried to hide deeper in her covers. The ring was so cold on her hand that her fingers had turned to ice. The bones clicked and clacked and rattled nearer.

The voice was hovering just over her head. "I've come for my ring," it breathed down on her.

Benjamin stood by the altar in the church the next morning. As the music of the wedding march began, he turned around and saw his bride. She was coming toward him down the aisle. Her beautiful dress trailed after her. Her face was covered by a lace veil. And the diamond ring sparked on her gloved hand.

All the fear and nervousness that Benjamin had been feeling fell away at that moment. He watched his beautiful bride as she slowly walked toward him and joined him at the altar.

The minister began the service. The music, the vows, the sermon — they all went by quickly. Then the moment came when Benjamin and Ellen were pronounced husband and wife.

"You may kiss the bride," the minister said, smiling at Benjamin.

Benjamin turned to his bride. He took her gloved hand with the ring sparkling on it in his.

The hand was cold, and so thin. Then he reached out with his other hand and pulled up the bride's veil.

And as he bent to kiss her, he saw her face — the grinning, bony face of the skeleton, staring back at him.

Poltergeist

Mariah had always had a wild imagination. So when she moved with her family into an old house in a new town, they didn't take everything she said seriously. At first. But after a while, they couldn't ignore what was happening.

Mariah's bedroom was on the second floor, just at the top of a curving flight of stairs. The very first night she slept there, a strange thing happened. She was lying under her sheets and blanket, almost dozing off to sleep. Then, suddenly, the covers were jerked down to the bottom of the bed.

Mariah lay there, shivering and screaming at the top of her lungs. Her parents ran into the room, wondering what had happened.

"Something was in here," Mariah stuttered in a shaky voice. "I was lying really quiet, and all of a sudden, somebody . . . something . . . pulled my covers off."

"Now, Mariah, that's just your imagination at work," her father said. "You probably kicked them off yourself while you were having a dream."

"No," Mariah whimpered. "It really happened. I heard a sound on the stairway right afterwards. Something is haunting this house."

Mariah's parents soothed her to sleep, but they didn't pay much attention to her story. Until the next evening.

The family was sitting around the fireplace reading after dinner. Mariah was reading a book about ghosts, her eyes getting wider by the minute. Suddenly a weird noise, almost like a mad laugh, came out of the fireplace. Then chunks of soot fell down the chimney, sending a cloud of black smoke into the room. As Mariah and her mother and father jumped up, coughing and choking from the smoke, another laughing sound echoed from the chimney.

"I know what it is," Mariah said. "It's a poltergeist, a mean kind of ghost that likes to play tricks and scare people. I just read about them. And I think one lives here."

Mariah's father didn't say anything. But he quickly doused the fire and shut the vent to the chimney. Whatever might be up there, he didn't want it to come down into the house.

The poltergeist left the family alone for a whole week. Mariah's parents decided that her idea about the house being haunted was nonsense after all. They tried to find other explanations for what had happened with the fireplace. It must have been a squirrel, they said.

Then the poltergeist struck again.

Late one night, there was a knock on the front door. Mariah's father walked down the stairway to open it. But no one stood on the doorstep outside — no one at all. Mariah's father shook his head and walked back up the stairs. As soon as he reached the top, the knocking started once more on the front door. He walked down again and opened the door. No one was there. But out of the darkness came a mad laugh, and the door slammed shut in his face.

Mariah had woken up and seen what happened. She saw the look of fear on her father's face as he climbed back up the staircase. With shaking knees, she crawled back into her own bed, pulled the covers up over her head, and held onto them tightly.

All was quiet. Then a tapping started on Mariah's window. At first it was so quiet that she thought it must be a tree branch blown by the wind. Slowly, the tapping grew louder and louder until it sounded like a desperate animal trying to get into her room.

Mariah tried to scream, but nothing came out of her mouth. She huddled under her covers, afraid to look at what might be outside the window. Then, suddenly, the tapping was inside her room. It started on her closet door, sounding like someone was inside trying to get out. Then it traveled around the room, along the walls, until it came to her bed.

TAP. TAP. TAP. RAP. RAP. RAP. The sound pounded into Mariah's brain. Soon it was only inches above her head. She screamed.

It was the loudest, longest scream her parents had ever heard. They rushed into her bedroom to find Mariah sitting straight up in her bed, her face pale and sweating.

Together they heard the mad laugh of the poltergeist fade away outside the window.

Mariah refused to sleep in her room anymore. Her parents couldn't bring themselves to argue with her. The poltergeist had gotten to them, too.

The next morning at breakfast, the family decided that they would have to move. No matter how much they liked their new house, they couldn't share it with the wicked poltergeist.

It took Mariah and her parents three days to pack up all the things they had moved into the house. But instead of being sad, they all felt happy that they were escaping. Mariah caught herself singing as she filled boxes with her books and clothes.

The moving van arrived on a Friday and loaded

up the family's belongings. That night, Mariah slept in a sleeping bag in her parents' bedroom. Every once in a while, she thought she heard strange sounds outside the window and up and down the stairway. But she just squeezed her eyes shut hard and told herself that after tonight, she'd never be bothered by the poltergeist again.

The next morning, the family had their last breakfast in the house and loaded their bags into their station wagon. Mariah sat in the backseat and turned around to look at the house one last time as her father drove down the lane. She raised her hand in a wave to the house and whispered, "Good riddance, you mean old poltergeist."

As she turned around to look at the road, a familiar, haunting laugh rose from behind her. Mariah heard the poltergeist's voice whisper in her ear.

"Where are we going?" it asked.

Horrorscope

Dana woke up that morning from a bad dream. For a second, she remembered what horror had jolted her from sleep. But then it slipped and slithered back into the dark sleep world of her mind. She lay in bed for several minutes, almost paralyzed by an overwhelming feeling of fear. What terrible thing had happened in her dream? What had left her heart beating fast and her knees weak with dread?

The alarm clock blared out music suddenly, breaking her thoughts. Dana looked and saw that it was 7:00. She had to hurry to get ready for school. She was a freshman in high school, and already she was feeling stress.

"Morning, Dana," her mother murmured as she blew on her hot breakfast coffee. "How did you sleep?"

"I had a bad dream," Dana answered, getting

herself a bowl of cereal. "It was gross. But I can't remember what it was about."

"You're just being superstitious again," said Mark, her younger brother. "A dream's not going to hurt you."

"Thanks for the advice," Dana answered. "But you don't have the problems I do now that I'm in high school. I've got two exams today and tryouts for the lacrosse team. No wonder I've got bad dreams."

Mark just ignored her and picked up the morning newspaper. He propped it up in front of his face and read the front page of the sports section.

Dana spooned her cereal into her mouth, thinking of all the problems she faced at school today. If only she hadn't had that dream. It cast a shadow over the whole day. Just then, she noticed the back page of the paper Mark was reading. At the top of one column was the daily horoscope. That was sure to cheer her up, Dana thought. Horoscopes were always full of suggestions for how you should act to make the day better.

"Let me have the back of the paper, Mark," Dana asked, reaching over for it. "I want to read the horoscope."

"Oh, come on, you don't believe in that stupid stuff," Mark mumbled from behind the paper. He made no effort to hand her the back section.

183

Dana shot a glance at her mother. Her mother sighed and then said to Mark in a stern voice, "Mark, share the paper with your sister."

Dana gave her brother a smirk as he handed over the back section that included the horoscope. Then she ran her eyes down to the listing she was looking for.

SCORPIO: Bad luck will stalk you today. Beware FHS 422.

A strange feeling swept over Dana as she read the horoscope. It was a feeling like déjà vu, when you sense you've experienced exactly the same thing before. But this wasn't déjà vu — it was a powerful sense of evil and fear.

"Dana, what's wrong? You're almost white. And you're trembling!" Her mother's voice drifted through her mind as though it were a hundred miles away.

Then there was a crash, and Dana felt a sharp pain in her right hand. She looked down to see blood oozing out of a cut on her palm. The table was a mess, full of broken glass from the milk pitcher.

"Mark, you clean up the table," her mother ordered. "Dana, let me put a Band-Aid on that. I can't believe you're so clumsy — even now that you're in FHS."

184

Dana winced when she heard her mother say the initials for Fairview High School. They had been in the horoscope. And following FHS was today's date — April 22, 4/22.

"I don't think I should go to school today, Mom," Dana said. "Something bad might happen."

"Nonsense, Dana. You know you have those two exams. You studied for them all last night. And what about lacrosse tryouts? You can't miss that. This cut isn't so bad."

"Okay, Mom," Dana said, knowing it was no use arguing with her mother.

"Now hurry upstairs, get your books, and start off for school," her mother said.

Dana ran upstairs to brush her teeth and comb her hair. She picked up a small hand mirror to look at the back of her head. But as she did, a wave of dizziness came over her. She lurched against the sink and tried to catch herself. The sound of the mirror cracking snapped her back to reality.

Mark looked in from the hallway.

"Seven years bad luck," he sneered. "You'd better be careful today, Dana. You're breaking everything in sight."

Dana stared down at the shards of broken glass from the mirror. Bad luck was stalking her today. And, suddenly, she was sure she shouldn't go to school.

"Dana, I'm sending you straight out the door to

school right now," her mother said as she put her arm around Dana and guided her out of the bathroom. "Now you get your books and start walking before you're late. I've got to get to work myself."

Dana grabbed her books from her room and followed her mother's directions. Mark ran ahead of her down the stairs and sprinted out the front door toward Fairview Middle School.

" 'Bye, Mom," Dana called out as she shut the front door behind her.

"Good luck on your exams and lacrosse tryouts," her mom called after her. "Tell me all about it when we get home tonight."

Dana forced her feet to walk one step at a time down the street toward the high school. Already, she couldn't remember the formulas she had memorized for the algebra test. And the lines from the poem that she was supposed to recite were a blurry confusion in her mind.

"Meow!"

Dana looked up sharply. A cat was standing in front of her on the sidewalk, its back raised up and its mouth open in a hiss. It was a black cat.

Dana stopped in her tracks as the cat slowly walked across the sidewalk in front of her and disappeared through a hedge. Her heart was beating fast again, and the words of the horoscope ran through her mind like a nightmarish echo.

Bad luck will stalk you today. Beware FHS 422.

Dana turned around and started to walk in the opposite direction from the high school. She couldn't go there today. She had to get away from all the crazy things that were happening to her.

The park where she had hung out as a kid was just ahead. Dana began to run toward it. It didn't matter if she cut school today. Only bad things were going to happen there anyway.

Without looking, Dana ran across the busy street that bordered one side of the park. Then she heard a loud honking noise and the screech of tires.

Dana looked at the car that was coming toward her. There was no way she could get out of its way. Frozen in terror, she watched the fancy grill and headlights hurtle toward her. And just at the last second, she saw the car's license plate. FHS 422.

It was the last thing she ever saw.

The Other Side

Ned and Jason were the only two boys who had to stay at school over the holiday weekend. Everyone else's parents had come to rescue them from Branston Academy for Thanksgiving. Ned lived too far away for his parents to come. Jason lived closer, but he might as well have been an orphan. His parents were always traveling. Over this Thanksgiving, they were in Africa.

On Thanksgiving Day, Ned and Jason joined the headmaster's family for a turkey dinner. Mr. Palmer, the headmaster, had two daughters. One was fourteen years old, like Ned and Jason. The other was just five. Kate, the older one, sat between the two boys at dinner.

"Have you seen the ghost yet?" Kate whispered during dessert.

Jason looked at her before answering. Was she serious or kidding? He wanted to impress her, for more than one reason.

"No, not yet," he said cautiously. He raised his eyebrows at Ned, who was listening.

"What ghost?" Ned whispered back.

"The ghost of one of the boys who went to Branston Academy," Kate said. "He died at school the day after Thanksgiving. He comes back every year around the same time he died."

"You're kidding, right?" Ned said.

Just then, Mr. Palmer cleared his throat and started to talk about the history of Thanksgiving. Kate and the boys had to listen and pretend they were interested. But as soon as they got up from the table, they went back to talking about the ghost.

"I'm not kidding," Kate insisted. "I think I saw the ghost myself when I was ten. I was up in the attic of your dorm, and I felt a presence. I saw something strange move across the room."

"Show us," Jason whispered, "tomorrow night."

"Tomorrow night," Kate agreed.

"I don't believe in ghosts," Ned said as the two boys walked back to their dorm. "I think she's just trying to make fools of us."

"No way," Jason said. "She said she might have seen the ghost herself. And it's not the first time I've heard this story. My older brother went here, too, and he told me the same thing."

"Yeah, right," Ned said. "I'll believe it when I

see it. But I don't mind spending an evening with Kate, ghost or not."

The next evening, the boys waited for Kate in their dorm, an old building that had been on campus for over a hundred years. The clock struck nine. Then ten. Then eleven.

"I told you this was just a joke," Ned said. "She was kidding us."

"Shhhh, I think I hear somebody," Jason whispered.

They both listened to the footsteps coming up the creaking stairs to their second-floor room. A few minutes later, Kate was standing in the doorway.

"Ready?" she asked, her eyes dark and serious.

Jason jumped to his feet. But Ned asked, "Ready for what?"

"We're going up into the attic," Kate said. "That's where I saw the ghost."

"The door to the attic staircase is locked," Ned said. "Anyway, we're not allowed up there."

Kate pulled an old key out of her coat pocket. "I know where my dad hides it."

"Let's go," Jason said.

The two boys followed Kate to the old door. The rusty key wouldn't turn in the lock at first. But finally Kate clicked open the lock, and the door swung open.

"Follow me," she said, starting up the stairs.

Jason went next, following with his eyes the beam of Kate's flashlight as it searched the darkness.

"Creepy," Ned said as the light picked out the old rafters and dusty cobwebs.

Kate walked straight toward the center of the attic and shone the light on a table there. "It's still here," she said in an excited voice. Jason and Ned hurried to where she stood and looked down at the strange board sitting on the table.

"What is it?" Ned asked.

"A Ouija board," Kate answered, "to call spirits."

Kate sat down and put her hands on the board. Ned and Jason sat down across from each other.

"What spirits?" Ned asked.

"The spirits of the dead," Kate answered. "You know, ghosts."

Ned looked over at Jason's face. It looked strange lit up by the flashlight. Jason seemed to believe all this stuff.

Kate kept staring at the Ouija board. "This is how you do it," she said. "You put your hands on the smaller board — that's a pointer. Then you concentrate and ask a question. The Ouija board will help you communicate with the spirit you want to talk to."

"But we don't even know his name," Jason said.

"I do," Kate answered. "His name was Oliver. Oliver Schuman."

Kate shut her eyes and placed her hands on the pointer board. Jason did the same. Ned sat watching them, wondering if he was the only sane one left.

"Oliver, can you hear me?" Kate asked in a low voice.

Ned watched as the small pointer board began to move across the Ouija board. Then it stopped, pointing to YES. Just then, the light flickered. And the flashlight rolled from the table and fell with a crash to the floor.

Everyone jumped. Ned bent down to pick up the flashlight and set it back on the table. He looked at Kate and Jason. They had both closed their eyes and still had their hands on the board.

"Oliver, come back," Kate said, pressing her hands onto the pointer. "Do you like where you are now?"

Again, the pointer underneath Kate and Jason's hands began to move across the board. It stopped at NO.

Kate and Jason's eyes flew open. They looked down at the Ouija board.

"He hears us," Kate said. "He just answered from the other side."

The hair was standing up on the back of Ned's neck. But he wasn't ready to believe in ghosts. Or spirits. Or Ouija boards.

"What are you talking about?" Ned asked in an angry voice. "What other side?"

"The other world. The world of dead spirits. The world of ghosts," Kate said. "Oliver traveled back from it to talk to us."

"Put your hands on the board," Jason said, looking hard at Ned. "Come on!"

Ned reached out his hands and saw that they were trembling. Quickly, he put them down on the Ouija board. The wood was warm where Kate and Jason had touched it.

Once again, Kate started to call to the ghost of Oliver Schuman.

"Oliver, come back. Cross from the other side. Are you near us?"

Ned felt a pressure under his hands. The pointer was moving again. He wanted to take his hands away. But he couldn't seem to move them.

"I feel his presence," Kate whispered with her eyes closed.

"I do, too," Jason said.

"No," Ned said. "He can't come back. Nobody comes back from the other side."

Just then there was a rumble of thunder not far away. Heavy pellets of rain hit the roof of the old attic.

"We shouldn't be here," Ned said, scared and wanting to go. "It could be dangerous being up here in this storm."

Kate and Jason ignored him.

"Oliver, can you talk to us?" Kate said in her low voice.

There was another rumble of thunder. The rain pounded down harder.

Ned watched as the pointer began to move across the board again. It seemed to be spelling out a word.

Then, suddenly, a flash of lightning filled the sky. Ned felt pain rip through his body. He felt as though every nerve ending inside him were on fire.

Everything went black for a long, long time. Then Ned saw light all around him. He reached his hands out into what seemed to be glowing clouds. He tried to touch Jason's and Kate's hands on the Ouija board. But nothing was there, just soft emptiness.

"Ned, can you hear us?"

"Ned, come back." It was Kate and Jason calling him.

Ned tried to answer them. But his mouth made no sound.

"Ned, can you hear us?"

Ned wanted to answer. But he didn't know how. He didn't know how to get back yet.

From the other side.

Good Luck Charm

Raymond slumped down in the backseat of the car. He didn't even have to look out the window to know what they were passing. Huge, spiny cactuses. Tumbleweeds rolling in the wind. And miles after miles of desert.

"Where are we going, Dad?" Raymond's sister, Felita, asked from beside him. Then she turned to Raymond and rolled her eyes.

"Same old place," her father answered with a grunt from the driver's seat. "You'll like seeing it again."

"Right," Raymond mouthed to Felita. They were both bored with going to the old mining town. It was the only place their father wanted to drive to when he got a day off from work. They lived in an apartment building in the city. Just once, Raymond wished they could go somewhere exciting.

Their father switched on the radio and began to

hum along with the music. Raymond hunched farther down in his seat and shut his eyes. He could see the mining town in his mind. A few straggling shops. A gas station. But mostly it was a ghost town now. Nobody wanted to live there anymore. It was no wonder.

"Think you'll see that old woman again, selling things?" Felita asked.

Raymond opened his eyes and looked at her. "I don't know. But I brought my money along."

"Don't waste it on her," Felita said. "That's just old, weird stuff she has."

Raymond shut his eyes again and started to think about what the old woman had spread out on her blanket the last time they were in the town. He didn't know why, but he wanted something from her. And today, he planned on getting it.

Raymond woke up as the car jolted to a stop. Looking around, he saw that they had arrived at the old town.

"You kids can walk around," their father said, turning around. "I'm going to talk to Miguel over at the store."

Raymond and Felita watched their father walk with a springy step to the old store where his friend Miguel worked. He would talk there for two or three hours. Then they would drive home again.

"Come on, let's stretch our legs," Felita said. "I'm going to run up to the hill that looks over the town."

"Go ahead," Raymond said. "I'll roam around here." He wasn't an athlete like Felita. She took off down the empty road at a fast jog.

Raymond got out of the car and started to walk down the dusty street. Most of the buildings were vacant. The old clapboard was peeling paint. Signs dangled crookedly from rusting nails. It was a ghost town, all right. Raymond got the chills walking through it sometimes.

Raymond turned to the left down the second alley he came to. That was where she had been last time — the old woman selling carved turquoise, strange-shaped rocks she found in the desert, and other odd things. His heart beat a little faster when he saw her there, sitting in the sun with a blanket spread out in front of her.

"Hi," Raymond said as he walked up to her.

The woman turned her wrinkled face up to him and stared at him with deep brown eyes. But she didn't say anything.

Raymond squatted down on the ground and looked over the objects on the blanket. He was glad Felita wasn't along. She said the woman sold strange things — things that were full of super-stition.

Raymond picked up an animal's skull that had been polished by years of being out in the desert. He turned it over and over in his hands.

"Coyote," the woman said to him. "Full of power. It will bring you strength."

Raymond laid the skull back down and fingered a snake skin. It was scaly and seemed strangely alive to his touch.

The woman reached down and picked up a small piece of turquoise. She put it in Raymond's palm.

"You could buy this as a gift," she said.

Raymond shook his head. He wasn't looking for a gift. He was looking for something to carry with him. Something that would bring him luck.

On the far corner of the blanket, he saw something he'd never noticed before. It was a rabbit's foot. As he reached for it, the woman grabbed his hand.

"What's wrong?" Raymond asked. "I want to see it."

The woman seemed to hesitate. Then she let go of Raymond's hand. He reached down and picked up the paw, which had gray fur and small claws at the end. It felt warm in his palm.

"How much is it?" Raymond asked.

"I can't sell it to you," the woman said. "It would be bad luck for me."

"But I want it," Raymond said.

The old woman picked up the paw and put it in Raymond's hand.

"Take it," she muttered. "But be careful."

Raymond stood up, holding the paw in one hand and stroking its fur with the other. He looked again at the woman and then ran down the alley to the main street.

His father and Miguel were sitting on the steps of the store where Miguel worked.

"What do you have there?" his father asked Raymond.

"A rabbit's foot," Raymond said, holding out the foot for them to see. "It's going to be my good luck charm."

Miguel's face screwed up when he saw the foot. "Did you get that from the old woman?" he asked.

Raymond nodded yes.

"You should throw it away, then," Miguel said. "She practices magic. That foot might still have the animal's spirit in it."

Raymond looked down at the paw. He wasn't going to throw it away. He looked at Miguel and shrugged and then walked away.

On the way back to the city in the car, Raymond turned the paw over and over in his hands.

"That's gross," Felita said. "I wouldn't carry around part of a dead animal. Anyway, maybe the animal didn't want its foot cut off. Did you ever think of that?"

Raymond looked down at the rabbit's foot. Suddenly it scared him. Maybe there was a reason the old woman had refused to take money for it. Maybe he should throw it away. But instead he pushed it down into his jeans pocket so Felita couldn't see it anymore.

Raymond started to close his eyes, but the sudden screech of the car's tires made him jump in his seat. He looked out the front window and saw a huge jackrabbit bounding across the road in front of the car. A second later, there was a loud, grinding crash, and everything went black.

"Raymond, Raymond, are you all right?"

It was Felita's voice, calling him out of the darkness that had drowned him. Raymond opened his eyes. Felita and his father were standing over him. Both of them looked very sad and very concerned. There were bright lights all around.

"What happened?" Raymond asked. "Where am I?"

"You're in a hospital," his father said. "We had an accident. It was that rabbit. It was crazy. It jumped in front of the car over and over again."

"It was so scary," Felita said, her voice shaking.

"It didn't leave after the wreck. Dad and I were okay. But you were lying on the ground. And the rabbit . . . it came up and pulled something out of your jeans pocket."

Raymond felt a shudder of fear travel through him. Then he looked away from their faces to the bottom of the bed. One leg was propped up and wrapped in bandages. He tried to wiggle his toes. But there was nothing to wiggle — nothing at all.

"That rabbit's foot," his father said. "You should have thrown it away. It was bad luck."

Moans from the Closet

The Wilton house was the most famous place in the old New England town. George Washington had actually slept there. The townspeople liked to brag about that. But they didn't brag about the horrible thing that had happened in the same bedroom Washington had slept in. They tried to hush that up. What weird old Mr. Wilton had done was a blotch on the house's reputation — one that just wouldn't go away.

Sam didn't like living in the small town. On long, hot summer days, there was nothing — absolutely nothing — to do. His mother had gotten bored, too, so she had volunteered to become a tour guide at the old Wilton house. The house brought a fair number of tourists into the sleepy New England town every summer. People came to see where George Washington had slept during one of the battles of the Revolutionary War. And while they were in town, they bought souvenirs, ice cream cones, food, and even watercolors from the art gallery.

Sam had liked the old Wilton house when he was little. He'd loved hearing stories about the first president sleeping there. But now he was a teenager, and George Washington didn't interest him much anymore. Nothing in the town interested him anymore.

"Why don't you come along to work with me today, Sam?" his mother asked at breakfast one morning. "Maybe you can help answer people's questions about the history of the house."

"Naw, that's okay," Sam said, his mouth half full of cereal. "That place is boring, except for the stories about old Mr. Wilton."

"You keep quiet about Mr. Wilton," Sam's mother said, her eyes flashing warning signals. "The mayor wants that whole story forgotten. Enough people still ask about him and the horrible thing he did. We want to give tours of a historic house, not a haunted one."

Sam didn't respond. He just kept eating his cereal. But in the back of his mind an idea was forming. An idea about how he could add a little excitement to the summer.

That afternoon, Sam walked over to the Wilton house, where his mother was at work.

"Come to see your mother?" asked the woman taking money at the door.

Sam nodded his head. He hated to lie, but it was the only way he could get in without paying. He knew his mother was working out in the back of the house this week, describing the house's herb garden and landscaping.

"Go ahead, then," the woman said. "We've got a good crowd today. Just don't bother any of the people who are taking the house tour."

Sam smiled to himself as he slipped through the door into the big sitting room on the ground floor. He wasn't going to bother anybody. He was just going to add a little excitement to the tour.

Sam sneaked around the edge of a group of people listening to the tour guide's lecture about the history of the house. He made a beeline for the staircase that led up to the famous bedroom. He knew that if he timed it just right, he could get there in between two tour groups.

Sam looked left and right as he reached the top of the stairs. Perfect. The tour group that had just visited the bedroom was now on its way down the servants' steps to the old kitchen. He crept quietly along the hall to the bedroom where Washington had slept.

No people were in the room. The big old four-poster bed with its blood-red comforter stood in the middle of the room. The bed had been there when Mr. Wilton had killed his wife. But it couldn't have been there when George Washington spent the night. Still, most of the furniture in the room was really old. The highboy dresser. The rocking chair where Mr. Wilton had patiently rocked, listening to his wife's moans as she slowly died in the closet.

Sam looked over at the small closet door, which was only four feet high. It wasn't really a closet — more like a storage place. He had gotten his mother to admit to him that it was where Mr. Wilton had locked up his wife. And it was where the police had found her body a month later.

Sam knew most kids would be afraid to get in that closet. But he wasn't. He didn't believe in ghosts. He just liked to make fun of people who did.

The sound of footsteps on the stairs echoed down the hallway and into the room. Sam knew he didn't have much time. He ducked under the velvet rope that kept tourists from roaming around the room and touching everything. Quickly, he pulled open the low closet door and crawled inside. It was a much smaller space than he had thought. But there was no turning back now. He crouched on the floor and pulled the door shut behind him.

Just in time. The tour guide came into the room making her presentation. She droned on about how George Washington had come to the Wilton house one stormy night during the Revolutionary

War. He had been given a warm bed in this very room. And on the small table, he had spread out his maps by candlelight and plotted his strategy for the next day's battle.

Finally, the tour guide paused and asked if anyone had questions. Two adults asked questions about the history of the house. Then Sam heard a younger voice pipe up.

"Wasn't this the room where Mr. Wilton killed his wife? Somebody told me to see the closet where he locked her up to die."

"Yeah, what about that?" another voice asked. "I hear both their ghosts haunt this place."

"I'm sorry," the guide said hastily. "We don't discuss that rumor. We're here to educate you about the house's important history."

Sam heard her footsteps start to leave the room. Other people began to follow her.

"I'll bet old Wilton stashed her in that little closet," a girl's voice said.

"I hear he laughed at her the whole time she was moaning and dying," another boy said.

"Come on, let's get out of here," the girl said. "Everyone else has gone."

Sam knew it was the perfect time. First, he let out a soft moan.

"What was that?" the girl asked.

Sam moaned again, a little louder.

"It's coming from the closet," the boy said.

"Come on, I'm scared," the girl hissed, her voice sounding panicky.

Sam listened to them run down the stairs. He laughed to himself. They probably thought it was Mrs. Wilton's ghost.

Sam tried to stretch out his legs, but the closet was too small. As he reached to open the closet door, he heard the sound of another tour guide's voice come down the hallway. Too late. He'd have to wait awhile to get out and stretch. Anyway, now he had another chance to scare somebody.

The next time he moaned from the closet, it was even better. An old lady actually started screaming. The tour guide came back up that time. He heard her walk over to the bed and probably look under it. But she didn't get near the closet. Maybe she was afraid of it, too.

The bad part was that he never got a chance to crawl out of the closet for the rest of the afternoon. And it was getting really hot in there. He couldn't move out of one position, and he was beginning to feel drowsy. So drowsy.

Sam woke up when he heard the sound of a latch sliding across the outside of the door.

"Hey," he yelled, trying to push the door open. But it didn't budge.

"Hey, let me out of here," he cried out. "I'm Sam Jarret. My mother works here."

207

No voice answered him from the other side of the door. There was no sound in the house at all. Sam wondered how long he had slept. Maybe all the tour guides and tourists had gone.

Then he heard the creaking sound. Creak. Creak. Creak. It was the sound of a rocker rocking back and forth, back and forth, across the old floorboards. Creak. Creak. Creak.

"Who's out there?" Sam yelled. He was beginning to feel desperate. He'd never been claustrophobic before. But this closet was getting to him.

Creak. Creak. Creak. The rocker just kept rocking.

Sam began to pound on the door. He was in a panic now. He didn't know who was out there in the room. But he knew he had to get out of the closet.

He pounded and yelled until he was exhausted. Then he stopped and listened. The creaking of the rocker had stopped, too.

Then the sound of the latch scraped against the old wood of the closet door. And, slowly, the door was pulled open.

An old man's face was staring at him, lit by the light from the candle he was holding. There was a crazed look in his eyes. Sam didn't have to ask Mr. Wilton his name. He knew.

The old man laughed and slammed the door back shut on Sam. Sam heard the latch slide shut again. And as Sam sat there in the dark, frozen in terror, he decided he believed in ghosts after all.

Meanwhile, Mr. Wilton's rocking chair creaked back and forth . . . back and forth . . . back and forth.

Too Late

Amy and I had been best friends since kinder-garten. We were always there for each other. But now all that has changed. Amy isn't the same person she used to be. It all began when the foreign exchange student came into her house. I knew from the start that he would cause something bad to happen. I tried to stop it. But I was too late.

I was sitting in my bedroom that afternoon when I got a telephone call from Amy.

"Jasmine, you've got to come over here. Now!" Amy's voice sounded breathless and a little scared.

"What's the matter?" I asked. I knew Amy exaggerated sometimes, and I was in the middle of a good book.

"He's here, the foreign exchange student my family is sponsoring. And he's so creepy. I can't stand it that he's going to be living in my house for the next three months!"

"I'll be right there," I said, and hung up the phone. I rushed out of the house and ran the four blocks over to Amy's house. When I got there, she was waiting for me on the porch.

"What's going on?" I whispered, trying to peer through one of the living room windows to see if I could see this guy who had Amy so upset.

"I told my mom that I didn't want him living here," Amy said in a trembling voice. "But she said she's made a commitment to the school. He's come all the way from Austria. We're stuck with him for three months."

"Well, if your mother thinks he's okay, maybe you're just imagining things," I said, trying to make her feel better. "Where is he?"

Just then the front door opened and a tall, thin young man walked out onto the porch. I can't really describe the feeling that came over me when I saw him. But I know that my blood started to run cold, because goose bumps rose all over my body. All around me, the air seemed to have changed and become thick and full of evil.

Amy cleared her throat uneasily and looked from me to him.

"Jasmine . . . this is Kurt Muller. Kurt, this is my friend Jasmine."

I met the cold blue eyes that seemed to be staring straight into my brain. I finally stuttered out a hello.

"Please tell your mother that I will be back for dinner, Amy," he said. "It was very nice to meet you, Jasmine." I smiled as he spoke to me in his polite, low voice. But when he smiled back, I caught my breath. His smile looked unnatural, like an animal baring his teeth.

"Do you see what I mean?" Amy hissed in my ear as Kurt walked down the sidewalk. "Isn't he creepy?"

"He's creepy, all right," I agreed. "But what are you going to do about it? Somehow you're going to have to put up with him for three months."

"Not if I can convince my mom to make him leave," Amy said. "Come inside. I want you to see his stuff."

We walked into Amy's house and bounded up the stairs. Amy and her parents slept on the second floor; Kurt had been given the third floor, which had been an old attic turned into a bedroom. Amy's older brother, who was now away at college, used to sleep there.

"Are you sure we should be doing this?" I asked as we came to the closed door to the attic bedroom.

"You've *got* to see this," Amy said as she pushed open the door. "He's not going to be back till dinner. You heard him say that."

I followed her into the low-ceilinged room, which was lit dimly by two small gable windows.

"It's over here," Amy whispered, suddenly sounding guilty. "I took a peek already when Mom drove him over to see the high school this morning."

I went over to the bureau where Amy was standing, staring at the objects that had been carefully laid out on top of it. The silver medallion hanging from a silken cord caught my eye first. I started to pick it up to study the strange inscriptions on it, but Amy caught my hand.

"Don't touch anything!" she warned. "I don't want him to suspect that I've been up here."

Beside the medallion was an old iron key, the kind you only see in movies set in old castles. And beside the key there was a thin book, bound in red leather. The writing on the cover was old-fashioned and ornate, and in a language I'd never seen before.

"What do you think it means?" I whispered.

"That's the problem," Amy said. "I have no idea. But it scares me."

I looked at her eyes that were troubled by fear, and I suddenly wanted to do anything I could to help her. I sure wouldn't want this creep staying in my house. And I didn't want him scaring my best friend, either.

"Run down to your room and get a piece of

paper and a pencil," I said. "Maybe if we can figure out what the words on this book mean, we can
get your mother to get rid of him."

Amy took off down the steps, and I looked
around the room some more. I opened the closet
door and saw his clothes hanging there. Most of
them were black — black turtlenecks and black
jeans. I knew other guys who dressed like that
sometimes, but not all the time.

Amy came back with the paper and pencil and I
took it from her to copy down the words on the
red book. It was harder than I thought. I couldn't
really tell what all the letters were because the
type was so strange and fancy. Just as I was fin-
ishing the last letters of the last word, a sound
floated up the staircase. It was the sound of the
front door opening.

I took one look at Amy's wide eyes and knew we
had to get out of there fast. We tiptoed to the door
and crept down the stairs to the second floor as we
heard the sound of his footsteps on the stairs leading up from the entranceway. My heart was beating so hard that it hurt by the time we reached the
second floor. Amy made a run for her bedroom and
I followed. I turned around just as I was shutting
her bedroom door behind me. He was standing in
the hallway, his cold blue eyes hard and his lips
drawn in a smirk. I slammed the door and sank
down on the floor.

"See!" Amy whispered. "He's horrible! I'm like a prisoner in my own house."

I looked down at the strange words I'd copied onto the paper. I didn't know how I'd figure out what they meant, but I knew I had to find out.

I took the paper with the book title on it to the library the next day. I searched through dictionaries and encyclopedias, but I couldn't find anything that looked remotely like those strange letters. Finally, I asked the librarian for help.

"Where did you get these words?" she asked with a puzzled look on her face. "I believe they're in some European language, but I'm not familiar with it."

"Uh, I found them on an old book," I said, stumbling over my words. I wasn't sure I wanted to admit where I'd gotten the book title.

"Maybe you can try the library at the university," she said, "if you can find a way there."

I knew that wouldn't be any problem. My mother taught at the state university in our town. But she was away on a business trip and wouldn't be back for three days.

I called Amy with my news as soon as I got home.

"I don't know how I can wait," she said, her voice sounding panicky. "Mom thinks I'm crazy for being so nervous about him. But it's so awful having him stare at me across the table at breakfast and dinner. I can't even eat anymore."

I heard Amy make a scared sound in her throat just then. She whispered into the receiver that she couldn't talk anymore and hung up. I knew why. Kurt must have come into the room. For a minute, I let myself think that Amy was just getting paranoid. But then I remembered how I'd felt around him.

The three days dragged by until my mom came home. Every day in school Amy told me stories of weird things that Kurt had done. I knew it was a long shot that the book title could tell us anything about him, but I had to find out.

Finally, Mom came home and agreed to take me to the university library. She even looked at the words I had written down, but said they didn't make any sense to her. Just before we left for the library that evening, I called Amy.

"How are you doing?" I asked in a worried voice.

"Not so good," Amy answered. "Mom has to go to a meeting tonight and Dad's away on a trip. I think I'm going to be left alone in the house . . . with him."

"Don't worry, I'll call you from the library," I said, "as soon as I find out what the book is about."

"Okay, but don't forget," Amy said shakily. "I'm counting on you."

The librarian guided me to a dusty corner of the reference room that was filled with old dictionaries in foreign languages. She pulled one from the shelf that had the same strange kind of letters on the front as the book had.

"Try this," she said. "It's a language from the old Hungarian empire. It was spoken in Transylvania years ago."

Transylvania. I couldn't remember why that sounded familiar to me. I started going through the dictionary, searching for the words. Slowly, I wrote them down, one by one.

A   Tasting   Guide   to   Human

My heart started to beat faster as I searched for the meaning of the final word. It was in the front of the dictionary. The fear that was forming in my mind grew and grew and finally came true as I found the final word.

Blood

With a cry, I jumped up and ran to the telephone. I punched in Amy's telephone number and waited with my heart pounding.

I heard the phone being picked up and a low voice answered, "Hello." It was him!

"I want to speak to Amy," I said, sounding desperate.

"She's right here," he answered, and I could see the horrible grin that must be on his face.

"Jasmine?" Amy's voice asked. To my surprise, she didn't sound scared at all.

"Amy, I found out what the book title is. You've got to get away right now."

"It's too late now," Amy said dreamily. "Too late."

She was right. I was too late. Amy lives in Transylvania with Kurt's family now. She pretends that she went over there as a foreign exchange student. But I know better.

Amy did leave me something to remember her by, though. The day she left, I found the thin red leather book in my mailbox. It was inscribed with my name. And blood type.

What a Night!

My friend Eve is a pain in the neck. Ever since she was a little kid, she's been afraid of the dark. I've tried to get out of her what happened to make her so scared. But every time I start asking questions, her mouth shuts as tight as a coffin lid.

But tonight I'm not going to take no for an answer. It's the big night of the year — the night when everybody is out. I'm not planning on sitting around like a moldy old corpse while everybody else is having fun on Halloween.

"No, I won't go!" Eve said stubbornly. She stared out the window at the dark violet sky. It was slowly deepening to a rich midnight blue.

"You've got to get over this," I said, looking into her green eyes. "If you don't face your fears, you're never going to get out and see the world." I gave her a wide smile, showing off my teeth.

"Besides, it's Halloween. Everybody is going to be out — even the little kids."

As soon as I mentioned Halloween, Eve shrank back into her favorite red velvet chair. I could tell from the look on her face that she was upset — really upset.

"Not Halloween!" she cried. "That's the worst night of all. People walk around in costumes. But underneath those costumes, you never know who they are. They might be somebody out to get you!"

"Oh, man!" I said with a sigh. It was beginning to look like another boring night hanging out in Eve's basement. I like this girl, but sometimes. . . .

Just then, I looked up through the high window in the room, and I saw a full orange moon rise over the treetops. It was so bright that it shone light down on everything like a yellow spotlight.

"Presto, no more dark!" I yelled and grabbed both of Eve's hands. I pulled her up out of the chair and pointed at the moon.

"Come on, there's nothing to be afraid of now. Old Mr. Moon will light our way."

Eve sort of whimpered like a little kid. I could tell she was still afraid. But my mood must have been catching, because a big smile slowly spread across her face, and the moonlight glinted off her beautiful teeth.

"You won't leave me alone, will you?" she asked.

"Cross my heart and hope to die," I said with a silly laugh.

Eve laughed, too, and I pulled her up the steps and out into the night.

We were dressed all in black, so it was easy to slip from shadow to shadow along the streets. We watched the kids running up to the houses, yelling, "Trick or treat!" The kids were older and bigger now that it was dark. Some of them even looked our age. So we knew no one would be suspicious if they saw us hanging around in the dark. It was so exciting that chills ran down my back. But Eve clung to my arm. She hadn't been out in so long that she was jittery.

"Come on," I whispered to Eve, "let's go up to some houses."

"No, let's just watch," Eve murmured. "I'm scared."

I decided that talking was going to get me nowhere. I grabbed Eve's hand and pulled her off down the street toward a big old house I had passed by many times at night. It had the spooky old look that I loved. I even had dreams of living there some day. I was sure it must have a really great old basement.

"Where are we going?" Eve asked.

"Just trust me," I said. "I've always wanted to

look inside this house. We'll pretend to be trick-or-treaters, and whoever lives there will have to answer the doorbell. Then I can look inside."

Eve didn't answer me, but I could tell she wasn't very happy. We passed by a couple of other teenagers on the street. When we smiled at them, they told us we had great costumes.

"Those kids were weird," Eve said. "Did you see the fake blood and tacky fangs they had on?"

"Yeah," I answered, "that blood looked disgusting."

We had gotten to the sidewalk that led up to the front door of the old house. It loomed up before us in the night, looking like the set for a horror movie. The roof was full of gables that jutted out, giving it a creepy silhouette against the night sky. The windows were dark except for one on the ground floor, where candlelight was glowing out into the night.

Eve followed behind me up the sidewalk to the door.

"Can't we just go home now?" she whispered. "I don't like this place. It gives me the creeps."

"That's what I like about it," I answered. "Just stay behind me. Nothing's going to happen to us."

I picked up the heavy iron knocker on the door and let it slam down on the old wood. Even I had to admit that it was pretty creepy. We waited for a couple of minutes. Then we heard footsteps coming toward us on the other side of the door. Heavy footsteps. A second later, the door swung open.

Everything hit us at the same time. The man's scary-looking eyes staring at us. The sight of the stake in his hand.

Eve's scream was so loud that it seemed to pierce my ears. I saw the man's eyes get even wider as he looked at her open mouth and shining teeth. Then he raised the stake toward us.

I turned around, grabbed Eve's arm, and started to run. She seemed to be frozen with fear, and I almost had to drag her down the front sidewalk. I could hear the man pounding down the sidewalk behind us. I could smell the garlic hanging around his neck!

Eve finally got her strength and started to run beside me. She was panting with fear.

"It's him," she sobbed as we ran. "He tried to get me years ago. I'll never forget those eyes!"

I looked over at her and finally realized why she hadn't wanted to come out all these years. Then I turned around and saw the man running after us — fast. He had the stake raised and his eyes were glittering with hate.

"Hurry up!" I yelled, pulling Eve faster. I saw some woods ahead that I knew like the back of my hand. On the other side was the place where I lived.

We ran into the thick woods, dodging between

the trees. The man's footsteps pounded after us. We could still smell the garlic on the night air. We kept on running as fast as we could. The woods were getting thicker and thicker. But I knew how to get through them.

"Come on, we've got to get some distance ahead of him so we can make a run for it."

Eve's sobs had turned into real tears by this time, but she kept running. Finally, the sound of the footsteps got weaker and weaker. And the smell of leaves overcame the horrible smell of garlic.

We made it to the edge of the woods and began to run through the graves. The moon was still so bright that I knew he could spot us if he got out of the woods before we made it.

With one last sprint, we got to the mausoleum in the middle of the cemetery. I pulled open the heavy stone door, pushed Eve through ahead of me, and then threw down the iron latch.

Gently, I opened a coffin for Eve to climb into. I wiped away the tears that streaked her face and touched the tip of one of her fangs.

"I promise I'll never take you out on Halloween again," I said before shutting the coffin lid.

Then I jumped into my own coffin and breathed a sigh of relief.

What a night!

The Third Wish

The day was hot — so hot that heat seemed to rise up from the sidewalks in wavy lines. James walked along, wishing he had a car like his friends. Ten days ago, he had gotten his driver's license. Not that it did him any good. His mother used the family car to get to and from work. His father lived in another state. That left James on the hot streets. Walking.

James had just come back from a job interview. He wanted to get a summer job to earn money for a car. But this interview hadn't worked out. Now he was in a strange part of town full of buildings with boarded-up windows and peeling paint. And he had to watch his feet as he walked to make sure he didn't stumble over the places where tree roots had pushed up the sidewalk.

So when James heard the man's voice call him from close by, he jumped.

"Hey, you're a little nervous, aren't you?" the

man said. When he grinned, James could see that several teeth were missing.

"No, not really," James said. He stared at the man sitting on the stoop of an abandoned building. The man was wearing ragged clothes and needed a bath, but there was nothing threatening about him. James knew it was best not to act afraid. Still, his heart was beating faster, and he really wanted to run.

"You wouldn't have an extra dollar, would you?" the man asked James. "I haven't had breakfast yet, and it's getting way past lunchtime."

James shook his head no. At the same time, he stuck his hands in his pockets to check for the twenty dollars in emergency money his mother had given him that morning. But it was just that — emergency money. She expected James to give it back.

"That's too bad. I sure could use a square meal," the man said. "I've been down on my luck for a while now, ever since I came across this so-called piece of magic."

James knew he should move on, but the word *magic* had caught his curiosity. He was reading a lot of books right now about strange, mysterious happenings. He wanted to find out anything he could about magic.

"What magic?" James asked.

The man stared James straight in the eyes for

several seconds. Then he pulled something smooth and white from inside his jacket. It was a bone, perhaps a small human finger bone.

"What's magic about that?" James asked. He wanted to touch the bone in the worst way.

"Someone down on their luck gave it to me," the man said. "It's magic, all right. It grants any wish you ask for. But I understand you can only have three."

"If it's so magical, why don't you wish for some money?" James asked.

"No, I've taken two wishes. And that's enough for me," the man said. "Might you be interested in the bone?"

James shook his head no. But he couldn't stop staring at the bone, lying in the cup of the man's palm. Three wishes. He could use those, all right.

"How much do you want for it?" James finally asked.

"How much you got?" the man said.

James felt in his pocket and pulled out the twenty dollars. He held it out to the man.

"You've got a deal," the man said, snatching the bill out of James's hand. "Just a few words of advice. Think hard about what you wish for. Everything comes with a price."

James wasn't sure what the man meant. All he cared about was getting the mysterious bone. Finally the man handed it over. It felt cool and smooth in James's hand. He turned it over and over, comparing its length and shape to his own finger bone. When he looked up to ask the man more about it, the man was gone. He'd vanished.

James walked the rest of the way home, lost in thought. What wishes would he make? One thing was for sure, he planned on thinking it through.

That night, when his mother asked for the twenty dollars back, James almost wished it was back in his pocket. But he caught himself in time and told his mother that he had lost it on the way home from the job interview. The lecture he got made him think about how much he wanted to be able to get away from home.

That night in bed, James settled on his first wish. He decided he wanted a new red convertible, just like the one his friend Brian had. Brian's family was filthy rich, and Brian got whatever he wanted.

James pulled the small white bone out of his pocket and in the moonlight solemnly wished for a red convertible — all his own.

The next morning, when James came down to breakfast, his mother was standing by the phone. She looked pale and frightened. The sound of the phone ringing was what had woken James up.

"Sit down, James," his mother said. "I've got some bad news."

James sat down with a feeling of dread growing in his chest.

"Brian died last night," his mother said in a shaky voice. "He was in a car accident — a freak accident. His red convertible was hardly scratched. But he flew out of his seat . . . and he hit the concrete. He stayed alive for only a few hours after they took him to the hospital."

A chill came over James as he thought about Brian. They went way back — to first grade.

"There's one more thing," his mother said. "Brian's parents want you to have his red convertible. They said Brian always knew how much you wished you had one."

Suddenly James felt sick. He jumped up from the table and ran to his room. The white bone was lying on top of his dresser. James picked it up and threw it into the back of a drawer. He didn't want to see it anymore. Everything had its price.

James didn't drive the red convertible for almost a month. Then one morning he woke up feeling as if a spell had been lifted from him. He grabbed the keys to the car and drove around town for three hours. He passed by a lot of kids from his class. Some looked at him funny, as if they thought he shouldn't be driving Brian's car. Others waved and seemed to remember how much Brian had loved the car, too.

James enjoyed every minute that he was in the car. But he wished somebody could share it with him. Like Molly. She had been in his class since elementary school, too. Their last names started with the same letter, and their lockers were always close to each other. Molly had been going out with Jess for half a year now. And since Jess was the only good friend that James had left now, he knew Molly was off limits.

Still, James couldn't get her off his mind. One night, he accidentally came across the white bone at the back of his drawer. Turning it over and over in his hands, he wished he could go out with Molly.

James woke up the next morning from a bad dream — a nightmare. He was almost afraid to pick up the phone when it rang. But his mother had already left for work. The phone rang and rang. Finally, he picked it up.

"James?" a voice choked with tears asked. "James, it's Molly. Jess died last night. Nobody knows why. I've got to talk about it — with you."

James listened to Molly as she talked about Jess between sobs. He felt as though he had turned to stone inside. As Molly went on about how much she had loved Jess, James stared at the white bone on his dresser. Just looking at it made him sick. He reached over and threw it deep into his drawer again.

A week passed. Jess was buried in the same cemetery as Brian. And Molly began to call James every evening to talk about Jess and how much she missed him. One night, Molly asked if they could take a drive together the next day in Brian's red convertible. James hung up on her and walked over to his dresser. He took the white bone from the back of the drawer.

Sitting on his bed, James turned the bone over and over in his hand. Then he made his third wish. He wished his friends would come back again.

James finally fell asleep, but he tossed and turned from bad dreams. In the middle of the night, he woke up — certain that he had heard the front door of his house open and close again. After that, he couldn't go back to sleep. He lay still as a corpse in his bed, waiting. Then he heard the footsteps on the stairs. Footsteps that slowly but steadily came toward his room.

James got up from his bed. He was sweating and scared. The footsteps moved down the hallway, closer and closer. Then the door creaked open and the overhead light flickered on.

They had come back. Brian and Jess. They stood in his doorway like two zombies back from the dead. Brian was covered with dried blood.

Jess's face was gray and swollen. They both stared at James with eyes full of anger and revenge. They knew.

James grabbed for the magic white bone. He squeezed it in his trembling hands and wished them to be gone.

But James had run out of wishes. Forever.

Teach Him a Lesson

Sam and Simon were as different as two brothers could be. Sam was fun-loving, irresponsible, and the black sheep of the family. Simon was serious, reliable, and the apple of his mother's eye. It was no surprise that the brothers didn't like each other.

During the summer that Sam was twelve and Simon was fourteen, things got really bad. The boys' father had to travel for a month on business, and they were left at home alone with their mother, whose nerves quickly unraveled.

"That Sam is driving me crazy," she muttered as she peered out the window, watching for Sam to come home. "Here it is, after dark already. He knows that his curfew is before dark. And he's late again — just like last night. That boy just doesn't obey!"

Simon sat quietly in the room, rearranging the books on the bookshelf so that they were all in

233

perfect alphabetical order by author. As he listened to his mother, he decided that it was time to teach Sam a lesson.

That night Simon devised a plan. He knew Sam was probably out hanging around town with his friends, up to no good. And to get home he'd have to walk along the dark lane that passed by the cemetery.

"Tonight," Simon thought aloud, "something will happen on Sam's walk home. Tonight I'll teach him a lesson he'll never forget."

Simon had never gone out after dark before, not alone. But he was determined that Sam wouldn't get away with what he was doing. After all, it wasn't fair that Simon should be so good and Sam be so bad.

Simon pulled the bottom white sheet off his bed and stuffed it under his arm. He had his plan all figured out. But he had to hurry.

The moon was just a thin sliver in the dark summer sky. Simon ran along the empty lane toward town. It was only a mile between their house and the town. Halfway between was the old cemetery, bordered by a stone fence.

When Simon reached the cemetery, he was already out of breath. His heart was pounding from the exercise he seldom got, and he could hear his breath coming in short pants. Looking out over the white tombstones in the pale moonlight made his heart beat even faster.

"You've got to teach him a lesson," Simon muttered to himself, partly to screw up his courage to the sticking point.

He scrambled across the low stone wall beside the lane and set his feet down in the cemetery. To his disgust, the ground was soft and seemed to sink beneath his shoes. Quickly, Simon walked toward a tombstone that was in the second row back from the lane. It was just high enough for him to be seen on it from the lane and wide enough to give him a comfortable seat.

There was a scuttling sound in the bushes by the tombstone as Simon walked up to it. His heart jumped into his throat, and for a moment he thought about running home. Running was out of the question, though. His legs were too weak from fear to move.

Finally, Simon forced himself to walk up to the tombstone and climb on top of it. He knew Sam would be walking by soon, and he intended to scare the living daylights out of him.

Simon wrapped the sheet around himself, leaving a narrow opening by his eyes. With icy fingers of fear tingling up and down his spine, he sat and waited for Sam to walk down the lane.

He didn't have to wait long. Sam came strolling down the lane, kicking a stone in front of him. He was humming a tune under his breath, as happy-go-lucky as he could be.

"I'll change his tune," Simon whispered to himself. He let out a low moan that floated across the cemetery on the summer air.

Simon watched with pleasure as Sam stopped short in the lane. Again, he let out a ghostly moan.

Slowly, Sam walked forward along the lane.

"Is that you again?" he called out into the graveyard.

For a minute, Simon stopped moaning, trying to figure out what his brother meant. Just nonsense, he decided, and let out another moan.

Sam walked a little nearer to where Simon was sitting on the tombstone. He peered straight into the cemetery, which was dark except for the pale moon that was shining off Simon's white sheet.

"Two ghosts tonight," Sam said with a nervous laugh. "There was only one of you last night."

The moan he was about to make caught in Simon's throat. He followed Sam's stare behind him in the graveyard. Sitting there, only two tombstones away, was a strange white figure. Its eyes stared back at Simon with a haunting, angry look.

Simon's scream echoed across the whole graveyard. He jumped up from his tombstone, threw off his sheet, and ran to the stone fence. As he leaped over it, he almost knocked Sam down.

"That should teach you a lesson," Sam yelled after him. "Never sit in a graveyard after dark!"

Trick or Treat

We always go out trick-or-treating together — me, my friend Jordan, Jordan's little sister Tessie, and Ruby, my next-door neighbor. There is no other day of the year that the four of us hang out together. But every Halloween, we meet at the corner by my house just when the sun is starting to sink in the sky. Over the years, we've gotten to know who is the bravest, the fastest, and the greediest. Ruby is always the greediest by far. She can never get enough treats.

So I guess you could really blame her for what happened.

This past year, I dressed up in a vampire costume that included fangs and fake blood. Jordan was a pirate, and Tessie was a little black cat. Ruby had on her old witch's costume, which was getting a little worn out. The peak of her black hat was bent over at the top, and her black witch wig was looking really weird.

We ran up and down the streets, ringing doorbells, screaming "Trick or treat!" and stuffing candy and sweets into our bags. By the time we had covered most of the neighborhood, it was dark. And we were at the farthest point away from our houses.

"I want to go home," Tessie started to whine. She always got tired first, but this year she had lasted longer than usual.

"I guess we've about covered every place anyway," Jordan said. He looked worried that Tessie was going to make a fuss.

Ruby was poking around in her treat bag, looking for her favorite kind of candy bar.

"We're not stopping yet," she said. "I've got less candy than I did last year. Every year we should get more than the last. That's my rule." Ruby talked in a way that made it hard to argue with her. We all started to walk in the opposite direction from home, not sure where we were going.

"We don't know this neighborhood," Jordan said after we'd gone about half a block. "Anyway, that old witch's house is around here."

I heard Tessie whimper a little. I could tell she was starting to get scared of the dark. I wasn't feeling too comfortable myself in the strange neighborhood.

"Look, there it is."

Ruby stopped suddenly and pointed her finger toward a house that was set far back from the sidewalk. We could see candles flickering in the two front windows, but bushes and trees hid most of the house.

I felt Tessie move closer between me and Jordan. "Does a witch really live here?" she asked.

" 'Course she's not really a witch," Jordan said. "Everybody just calls her that."

"Listen, Ruby," I said, looking around at the deserted sidewalk, "let's just go on home. There aren't any other kids trick-or-treating on this block. You can have some of my candy if you haven't got enough yourself."

"No, I want to go up to this house," Ruby insisted. "I'm not afraid of the old lady who lives here."

Ruby pushed open the low iron gate that separated the yard from the sidewalk and started to walk up the brick path that led to the house.

I looked at Jordan and shrugged my shoulders. It was too late to talk Ruby out of doing it. And we'd never live it down if we were too scared to go up with her.

"Come on, Tessie," I said, taking her hand. "There's nothing to be scared about."

Tessie sniffled a little bit, but followed us as we walked behind Ruby to the house.

"I wonder what she'll look like?" Jordan whispered.

"Long yellow teeth," Ruby whispered back. "A big hook nose. Black hair down her back."

Tessie really started to cry then. Jordan had to pick her up and carry her the rest of the way to the porch.

We stood on the porch in front of the door and waited after Ruby knocked. Nobody came. Ruby knocked again. The candles were still flickering in the windows, but the rest of the house was dark.

Then, all of a sudden, a light went on inside, and the door opened wide. We were blinded by the light for a few seconds. Then we saw the old woman standing in the doorway. She had her gray hair put up in a neat bun. Her eyes were blue, her nose was normal, and her smile was kind and inviting. Best of all was the tray of candy, cookies, and other goodies that she held in her hands.

"Trick or treat," we all said, sort of nervously.

Ruby reached her hand out to grab some of the candy off the tray, but the woman stepped back into the room before Ruby could take any.

"Come in," the woman said in a soft, sweet voice. "So few children knock on my door anymore. And I just love to welcome trick-or-treaters into my house. Let me see your costumes."

I followed Ruby and Jordan and Tessie into the house, even though my mother had given me a strict lecture never to go inside anyone's house on Halloween. But I felt silly to worry about this old lady. She couldn't be a witch. Never in a million years. She looked like the nicest grandmother in the world.

"Now, let's see, you're a pirate," the woman said, looking at each of our costumes, "and you're a cat. You're a vampire, and you," she paused as she looked at Ruby, "you're a witch."

I thought I heard her voice get a little harder and colder when she said the last word. But before I could think about it, she was offering us the tray of candy and goodies.

Ruby took two pieces of candy and a little bag of cookies and stuffed them into her bag. We all helped ourselves, and the woman just smiled and offered us more.

Ruby picked up a piece of licorice and started to bite off the end.

"No, no," the woman said sharply. "Don't eat anything in the house. Wait until you reach the sidewalk outside the gate."

Ruby lowered the licorice from her mouth and stared at it hungrily.

"But take the rest of the candy," the woman said with a smile. "Put it in your bags. I'm sure you'll be my last trick-or-treaters of the night."

So we took it all, stuffing our bags with every shape and size of candy until they were heavy.

"Happy Halloween, dearies," the old woman said as we filed out the door. "And remember, don't eat anything until you go through the gate."

Ruby was walking first down the brick path, and she was still carrying the piece of licorice. I saw the greedy look in her eyes as she stared at it. We were still on the path when she put it up to her mouth.

"Ruby, don't eat it," I said.

Ruby wouldn't listen. She put the licorice in her mouth. Suddenly she started to scream. She stood there in the moonlight screaming and screaming. The rest of us saw the licorice twist and turn in her hand. Then Ruby threw it down on the ground. We watched in horror as a snake raised its head and hissed at Ruby. Then it slithered off into the night.

Finally, Ruby stopped screaming, only to start again when the bag of candy in her other hand started to twist and turn. When she dropped it, it hit the brick path with a funny, squishy sound. We all jumped back as the bag flopped away into the bushes.

"Drop your bags!" I screamed to everyone as I felt mine begin to squirm in my hands. We all threw the bags into the grass and bushes and watched as they wiggled and squirmed away.

Ruby was the first one through the gate. We all ran after her down the sidewalk. We ran and ran. But we couldn't escape from the witch's evil, cackling laugh. It followed us all the way home.